SERIES

T0339818

After the tears

Michelle Faure

cover2cover
books

Also available in the Harmony High series
Broken promises
Sugar Daddy
Jealous in Jozi
Too young to die
Two-faced friends
From boys to men

Published in South Africa by
Cover2Cover Books
cover2cover.co.za
Copyright © Cover2Cover

First published 2014

ISBN 978-0-9922017-8-4

Cover and book design: Robin Yule
Typesetting: Robin Yule
Cover models: Phumza Kibi and Bongimpilo Mondlane
Cover photo: Sue Kramer
Series editors: Dorothy Dyer and Ros Haden
Editing: Sandra Dodson and Sean Fraser

Acknowledgements

Thanks to Nosiviwe Lutuli, librarian at Masiphumelele Library, and also to Esethu Mngxunyeni and Bulela Mgoqi from LEAP Science and Maths School, Cape Town, for their helpful feedback on this book.

Chapter 1

It was a stormy Saturday afternoon. Busi sat alone in her grandmother's armchair, holding her stomach as if to protect the baby growing inside her. The light was dim as she watched the rain pelting down outside. It had been raining all week and their shack was leaking. The bucket she had placed below the most rusted section of the corrugated-iron roof wasn't much help. Everything was damp and cold and uncomfortable. The *plop … plop … plop …* of the water droplets hitting the bucket made it hard to sleep at night; that and the cough that racked her granny's thin, frail body.

Sleepless nights made Busi so tired and depressed that she could hardly concentrate at school and her marks were slipping. If she didn't make a big effort now, she wouldn't pass Matric. But somehow the weekends, when her friends were out having fun without her, were even more depressing than weekdays. It was not like they didn't invite her along. The truth was that when she was with them, surrounded by their laughter and listening to their holiday plans, she felt even worse – like a stranger, even to herself. She knew what she would be doing in her holiday: she would be looking after a baby. Her life was about to change forever, while they would go on being young and carefree. No, it was better to be alone sometimes.

Just then Lettie's SMS popped into her inbox:

> Cum join us. Talkin bout matric
> dance plans
> LX

Busi quickly replied:

> Nxt tym

Then she pressed SEND.

She was going to put the phone down, but she hesitated. Instead she started scrolling through her old messages until she found it: the first ever SMS she had got from Parks:

> Hey babe – had the best time –
> EVA

It was strange to remember the thrill she felt when she first received it, when Parks was still the cool older guy paying her compliments, not the father of her baby. The SMS had popped into her inbox the evening of the day she met him, the day she jumped out of that broken window at school and he drove by in his taxi, Loyiso booming out of the speakers … and she had climbed inside. The beginning of their affair seemed so long ago now.

Her heart still skipped a beat when she read it. But almost instantly she was filled with sadness. Her Sugar Daddy Parks – oh so sweet in those first months – taking her to fancy restaurants, buying her gifts, treating her like a princess. Why had he turned so sour and angry when she fell pregnant – even angrier when she refused to have an abortion?

Now all she had were his old SMSes. She should have deleted them, wiped him out of her life completely – that's what her girlfriends and Unathi had urged her to do. But she just couldn't. Not yet, when there might still be a chance. For what? For him to leave his wife?

Lettie had shaken her head. "Never. Give it up, Busi. Why would you want him back, anyway, after how he treated you?"

Even though she knew it would upset her, she made herself read his last SMS. It still made her shudder:

Get rid of the baby. Just do it.

Then silence.

The nice Parks who had loved and spoilt her had disappeared completely. Instead that horrible

Parks was out there somewhere, wanting her baby gone. She was alone and vulnerable. If only her mom were here to protect her, not so far away in Jozi. Her granny needed protecting too. There wasn't even a proper lock on their door. If Parks wanted to get in it would be easy.

Busi looked out at the rain again. She tried to slip her cell phone into the pocket of her jeans, but she couldn't do it any more, even though they were stretch denim – she was gaining weight by the day. The top button had to be undone now and she had to wear long, loose shirts and tops pulled down to cover the large safety pin that kept the zip from slipping down.

Busi closed her eyes, and leant back her head. She just wanted to escape into sleep, to curl up under a blanket and forget about everything. She was beginning to nod off when the door banged open and icy rain swept in on the winter wind. Seeing her grandmother in the doorway, wrestling with a buckled umbrella and a large bag of groceries, Busi leapt up. Jumping over the puddle at the door, she grabbed the umbrella and held it over her granny while she stepped inside.

"You should have woken me this morning so I could come with you," said Busi as she shook the umbrella and closed it.

The harsh wind cut into her face.

"Come, shut the door quickly," said the old lady, tugging on Busi's arm with her thin, frail hand.

A moment later the women had managed to secure the door shut. They stood facing each other, the young and the old, shaking off the raindrops. Busi shivered. The rain had drenched her in a matter of seconds.

"The shops are far and you need your rest," said Busi's granny, putting down the shopping bag and walking slowly towards the armchair.

Busi helped her grandmother out of her navy blue coat and plumped up the cushions as the old lady eased her aching body into the chair. Then she bent down to remove her granny's sodden shoes from her feet and rubbed them dry with a towel. Her grandmother's feet were gnarled and small. How could they keep walking the distances they did every day? She looked up at her grandmother with concern. What would I do if Gogo got sick now, or even died, Busi thought anxiously.

"I'll make you a cup of tea," said Busi, turning to light the gas and putting on the kettle. She tried to control the wave of fear as she poured out two hot cups of tea and ladled in the five spoonfuls of sugar she knew her granny liked. Her granny was the only person she had right now. What if something happened to her? "Here you are, Gogo," she said gently, placing the cup on a table nearby.

"Thank you, my child," said her grandmother, taking the hot cup between both her hands to warm them. Then, after a moment, she added, "Have you heard anything more from your mother?"

Busi shook her head. Her mother had promised to come for the birth. But it was right now that she needed her. Her tea tasted bitter, like the disappointment that she felt.

Her grandmother sipped her tea slowly and smiled weakly at her. "You must not worry too much, Busi," she said softly. "Your mother will come. She will be here when the baby is born."

Busi looked away, frowning, trying to stop the tears from coming. Even my own mother is not here for me when I need her, she thought angrily.

As if reading her thoughts her grandmother spoke again. "Your mother is my daughter, Busi. And I know her. If she is not here there is a good reason. Perhaps she will lose her job if she comes now. She is strong and good. Just like you are. You will be that kind of mother. Don't lose hope. She will come."

Busi stood up. She didn't want to hear any more. She excused herself, saying that she was tired and wanted to lie down. On her bed, behind her curtain, Busi let the tears roll down her cheeks. She closed her eyes and there was Parks with that smile and that look in his eye that had made her heart beat faster. She remembered the sensation of his firm, warm lips on hers. She remembered the feeling of his hands running over her body, touching her most secret and hidden places.

But then she remembered the nights in the sleazy hotels and that other Parks: the crazy Parks who had screamed at her when he found out she was pregnant, the Parks who had dropped her at the doctor to have an abortion and then driven off, leaving her alone. She could see him smiling down at her, then sneering at her, sharing a joke with his wife about what a silly little girl she was. And when those unwanted thoughts came rushing in, tears came too and Busi let them. She could taste them, bitter and salty on her lips.

"You stupid, stupid girl," said a voice in her head, over and over again. It was her inner voice, the voice of regret, but it echoed the voice of Parks. It belonged as much to her as to him. Where was he now?

Chapter 2

The papers in the street whipped around Busi's ankles as she battled against a stiff north-west wind on her way to Harmony High. She bent her head and tugged at the large school jersey she was wearing, pulling it down over her trousers and the zip that she could barely close.

When she went through the school gate a group of girls was waiting for her. But they weren't her friends, wanting to know if she was OK after the weekend. No, it was Princess and her 'groupies' who seemed to be waiting for her around every corner, poking fun with their bitchy words.

"Hey, girl, no one to give you any fun any more," Princess said.

"Nah, she's given all she's got, and it obviously wasn't enough to keep him," the other jeered. They all laughed.

"Shame, at least she's got something to remember him by when she gets lonely in the night," Princess said. "A little baby that will make her fat and old before her time, so no one else will look at her."

Busi knew the girls loved to be mean to anybody they could get their claws into, but the words hurt her nevertheless. She tried to ignore the remarks, but the girls didn't let up with their cruel teasing. "I hear that …" Zikhona started saying.

"Busi!"

She looked up with relief. There were her dear friends coming towards her. The girls behind her melted away. "Hey, you didn't come to Asanda's."

Busi shook her head. "There's lots on my mind. I'm sorry."

"So you've made a decision to keep the baby, then." Lettie's voice was serious now. They were huddled together against the wall, trying to get warm against the red bricks of the school building.

"*Hayi*," said Asanda, frowning at Lettie, "ignore her, Busi. It's not her business."

Lettie shrugged and added, "It's pretty obvious, isn't it?"

Busi looked up sharply, her hands flying to her stomach.

"Oh, sorry!" said Lettie as she realised

what she had said, "No, it's not obvious at all, Busi. Not that way, I mean. You don't look any different at all." Lettie turned to Asanda and Ntombi, "Does she, girls? She still looks slim and ..." Lettie's voice trailed off.

Asanda and Ntombi shook their heads.

"Why don't you just shut up, Lettie?" said Asanda.

"Yes," agreed Ntombi, "you're just opening your mouth to change feet!"

Busi looked around at her three friends and shrugged slightly. "It's OK," she said awkwardly. "It's OK, you guys. I understand what Lettie was trying to say."

The group of friends huddled closer to escape the wind.

Lettie looked up at the grey sky and frowned, "And now I suppose it's going to start raining in a minute." She reached over and put her arm around Busi's shoulders. "You're really going to have to start looking after yourself now, Busi," she said with a gentle smile. "It's not just you any more."

"Yes," said Ntombi, reaching out and touching Busi's hand, "and we're all here for you, Busi. I hope you know that."

Busi nodded gently. "I do know that," she replied softly. "Thanks, guys." But inwardly she knew that, however much they reassured her, they couldn't know what it was like being pregnant. She was on her own.

The group stood in silence for a moment, until they felt the first cold raindrops falling heavily on their backs.

"Run!" said Lettie, breaking free from Busi and running towards the shelter of the classrooms.

Asanda and Ntombi shrieked and turned away, putting down their heads to follow her across the school yard. Busi hesitated for a moment. She looked up at the sky and paused. Raindrops beat down on her cheeks and she closed her eyes, imagining she might be able to wash herself away. The school yard was rapidly turning to mud. She stood and watched her friends as they leaped over brown puddles, screeching and laughing and splashing. She could feel herself getting drenched, but she stood quite still and watched them as they ran away from her.

"Busi, come on. You're going to get soaked!" said a voice close by.

Busi turned. "Hey, you."

It was Unathi, pulling his anorak off and throwing it over her shoulders.

"Don't worry – I'm OK," said Busi as he did

so. But Unathi had her firmly by the arm and was tugging her along with him. The rain had started to pour down forcefully, and Busi had no option but to run with Unathi, her feet sliding and skidding in the mud. She almost slipped, but Unathi caught her in his tight, comforting grip.

"Thanks," said Busi, giving Unathi his anorak when they got inside.

He smiled at her. "You coming to the hip-hop session today? Some of us are performing at the end-of-term party."

"Oh, I don't know," she said. "Maybe ..." She didn't notice the look of disappointment on his face as he slung the anorak over his shoulder and walked into his Science class.

Her three friends were already in their English class, helping each other to dry off their hair. They were laughing and giggling and chasing each other around, flicking water at each other. The sexy, handsome Themba came over and Lettie pressed herself against him before the teacher came in. They looked so happy together, so in love ... He was a real catch.

Busi slipped quietly into her seat and wiped her hands over her damp cheeks. She turned her back to them and their jokes. "They don't even notice me," she thought to herself. "And why should they? They are all still so trouble-free. Why would they want to take on all my troubles? They are all just being kind." She leant forward and put her head on her hands, lifting it only when she heard the teacher come in.

"Quiet now," said Mr Khumalo's stern voice. "Take your seats and take out your books. You have exams coming up. Goodness gracious! One would think none of you had ever seen rain before!"

Gradually the class settled down and Busi opened her text book. Looking up she caught Mr Khumalo staring at her. She knew her grandmother had already been to see him. He had agreed that Busi could stay on at school for as long as she could.

Busi held Mr Khumalo's gaze for a moment. His eyes were steady and clear as he looked at her. There was no hint of a smile. His face was closed and still. Busi was the first to look away. She felt her cheeks grow hot and she fumbled with her pencil. She remembered sitting in his office, trying to tell him about Parks. "He drives around looking for young schoolgirls. I–he–" she had stammered.

"Let me get this clear – you are telling me that you went off with a grown man on your own, without knowing who he was?" He had looked at her as if she was mad. She had wanted to fall through the floor.

But he had listened, and told her that he would tell the teachers to look out for Parks's taxi. It was all they could do. Then she had got up to leave. He had started looking at papers on his desk, and did not answer her quiet "Thank you" as she pulled the door closed behind her.

She was jolted back to the present by the siren sounding for the end of the day. She managed to escape through the school gates before her friends could catch up with her. She wanted to be alone. But as she turned the corner she stopped in her tracks. Wasn't that Parks's taxi with DJ Ganyani pumping from the speakers? She looked for the *gaadjie* in the back. But then the taxi pulled away from the curb. She turned quickly and ran until she was safely in the next street. She hoped he hadn't seen her in his rear-view mirror. If he had, he would come looking for her, asking if she had got rid of the baby. What would she say?

Chapter 3

As Parks drove back up the street towards Harmony High he pulled his cap lower over his eyes and turned down the music. He didn't want to draw attention to himself. The security guard was walking up and down outside the school. It wasn't safe to drive past Harmony High any more. Word would have got out about what happened to Busi, even if she hadn't told the principal herself. Rumours spread faster than a sex clip on YouTube.

He needed to see Busi. He needed to know. Was she pregnant? If she was she would be, what, four months by now? When had they had sex for the first time in that Formula One hotel? The thought of her being pregnant made him feel sick. Why hadn't she had the abortion when he had arranged everything? And how had Thandi found out that Busi was pregnant? His wife had a way of finding out about everything – it was like she was following him everywhere, breathing down his neck. Now she wanted to know if Busi had got rid of the child. She had warned him: "Another girl, Parks, and you're out on the street."

"Never, again," he had said, and begged for her forgiveness. "You are the only woman in my life now." On uttering those words, he'd almost believed them.

At the stop street he turned left, away from the school. And suddenly there she was, ahead of him on the road. He couldn't call her; there were too many people about. Damn! He slowed down and pulled over.

She was wearing a thick yellow winter jacket over her school uniform. If it were summer it would be easier to see if she was pregnant. But there was no way he could tell now.

He watched as a tall, thin boy ran up to her. Busi greeted him and they walked together around the corner into the next street.

"If you ever see that girl again, or any other 'young bitch' for that matter, you will regret the day you were born." That's what his wife had said after she'd found out about Busi. If only Thandi wasn't the one with all the money. And she owned the house. He had nothing without her – that was the truth.

His cell beeped. Here she was now, checking up on him. Every minute.

Buy champagne for anniversary
tomorrow – remember?

How could he forget …? It had been 12 years of her tears and rages. Twelve years of spending her money, but also saving her from the trouble she had got herself into. Twelve years of her commands, making him feel like he was nothing. How could a man live like that?

That's what had driven him to cruise outside high schools in his taxi. That's what had driven him to drive past Harmony High and to stop when he saw a pretty girl. Busi wasn't the only one – although of course that's what she thought. It was what all the girls thought. He sighed as he remembered the first. Pity her father had caught them together, and threatened to break his legs.

Busi hadn't had a father, well, not one who was around. Just an ancient grandmother who couldn't protect herself, let alone her grandchild. It had been easy.

Taxis drove past full of school kids screaming and laughing. He watched as the last groups of kids walked past on their way home. He was about to start the taxi and go to the bottle store for the champagne, when he looked in his side mirror and saw a girl walking alone on the pavement towards his taxi. She was pretty and petite and there was something in the way she swung her hips that made him excited.

He wound down the window. "Hey, pretty girl." He flashed his most charming smile.

She stopped and smiled back.

"How would you like some airtime?"

She hesitated. He knew what she was thinking. For what in return?

"I need some information. Just something small …" He held up the airtime voucher. He had a whole pile of them in his cubby hole.

"So what do you want to know?"

"Do you know a girl called Busi?"

She laughed. "Which Busi? There are many at school."

"She's in Matric. She lives off Banda Street with her granny."

"Oh, that Busi! Yes, everyone knows that Busi – the one who got herself pregnant by a Sugar Daddy." She laughed, like she knew Parks could be that Sugar Daddy.

"Is she still at school?"

"Yes, but I'm not sure for how much longer. It's beginning to show, you know. You can't use a safety pin forever …"

"Thanks." He winked at her. "You're really pretty, you know. What's your name?"

"Asisipho."

"Maybe we'll meet again, Asisipho? Maybe you'd like some more airtime?"

He watched as she walked away, swinging her hips … So it was true. Busi was still pregnant.

⌘ ⌘ ⌘

Busi had just said goodbye to Unathi. She was nearly at her gate when Lettie ran up, skipped over a puddle and took her by the arm.

"So?"

"So what?"

"Unathi walked you home?"

"Yes … what about it?"

"I always thought that you two would make a good couple …"

Why would he want a pregnant girlfriend, Busi thought. Really, Lettie said the stupidest things. It wasn't like Busi had never thought about it. But then she had quickly thought about all the reasons why it would never work. There wasn't that chemistry she had had with Parks. Unathi didn't make her heart beat faster.

"But he's kind and he's funny," Ntombi had told her in the past.

"And he's hardworking; he's going places, chommie," Asanda had added.

That was true – Unathi was so kind, and entertaining as well. He could make people laugh. But she needed him as a friend. If you went out with guys they could dump you, and then there was never any going back to being friends. She didn't want to risk that.

"Well ..." Lettie looked at her. "We're all going to Asanda's this afternoon to talk about what we're gonna do after exams, and also about the Matric dance. Hlengiwe is going to help Ntombi put in extensions. You know how good she is at it." She smiled. "Oh, it's so great the exams are just about over."

Busi said nothing. She had hardly worked for these exams – they had meant nothing to her, and she knew she had probably failed them. And, anyway, what was the point of talking about the Matric dance if she wasn't going to go? By the time of the party there was no way she would be seen dancing.

Lettie chattered on happily. "And do you know Themba's been accepted for tech next year? And Ntombi and Olwethu had a fight, can you believe it? Those two love birds ..."

"That's a first!" said Busi. She was surprised. Olwethu was the perfect boyfriend. But that's what couples did – they fought, they made up.

"And remember that guy Mandla, the one who's so good at singing? He's coming around too – he's in a band, and they might play for the dance. Asanda liked him even when we were in primary school. You remember, don't you?" Lettie paused for a moment, hardly waiting for a reply before continuing, "Anyway, she sent him a message, and he replied! He said that he would see her."

Lettie's voice faded into the distance. Busi had stopped listening. She was lost in thought. Primary school. That seemed like a million years ago. She no longer cared. She didn't care about Asanda and Mandla or about parties or school. What Lettie was talking about was children's stuff. Just children's stuff! Busi's breath caught in her throat. For a moment she felt like she couldn't breathe. It was like a weight was pressing down on her chest.

"Busi?" said Lettie, pausing in her chatter to look at Busi, "Are you all right?"

"I'm fine," said Busi, opening her gate. "Just tired."

"So, will we see you later?" asked Lettie, smiling broadly, like the sun after the rain.

"What?" Busi couldn't concentrate. She had just heard her cell phone beep with a message.

"Asanda's place," Lettie reminded her. "Extensions. Remember?"

"Oh," said Busi, turning away and walking towards her front door. "No, I don't think so.

Not today."

Busi fumbled to get her key into the lock of her front door, hardly looking back to say goodbye. When she was inside she looked down at her phone and her heart gave a jolt.

Parks.

She put her phone down on the table. She couldn't bear to read the message. Not yet. What was he doing SMSing her after all this time? She was too nervous to read it. She would make tea. She would force herself to wait. But as she poured the water into the kettle her mind was racing.

What if he wanted her back? What if he had decided that he really loved her after all? And that he was going to divorce his wife and be with her, Busi, happily ever after? What if? She stirred sugar into her tea. There wasn't much sugar left and it had been the last teabag. They had run out of the latest shopping so quickly. What if Parks still wanted her to have an abortion? What if he was angry with her? What if? Busi sat down with her hot cup of tea and picked up the cell phone. Hesitantly she clicked on the message and waited as the text filled the screen.

I hear u still pregnant – is it true?

Chapter 4

"And …?"

No sooner had Parks walked in the door than Thandi started with her questions.

"Did you find out? Is that little bitch pregnant?"

He walked to the drinks cabinet and poured a whisky into one of the new crystal glasses Thandi had ordered. She bought things all the time. It was like there was a dark empty hole inside her that she was trying to fill with things – new things, expensive things. But that hole was too deep – it could never be filled, no matter how many things she bought.

"Is the girl pregnant?" Thandi asked again.

Parks nodded. He had thought of lying, but she always found things out in the end. He was surprised when his wife did not look angry. Far from it. In fact she looked pleased.

"You saw her?" she said. "You saw she was really pregnant?"

"No … I mean yes, I saw her, but I couldn't

tell."

"What do you mean, you couldn't tell?"

"It's winter. She was wearing a thick jacket over her school uniform."

"You spoke to her?"

"Not to her … to another girl. But everyone knows at school … "

"You spoke to another girl. I told you!" Her voice started rising.

"It's not what you think. I asked her about Busi."

Parks poured another large whisky and filled up the heavy-bottomed glass with soda for his wife. He brought it to her as she sat on the couch.

"She told me that Busi was pregnant," he mumbled.

"And you are the father …"

Parks sighed inwardly. Here we go again, he thought.

But then she stopped talking, did not rant on as she usually did. She stretched out her legs on the couch. Parks squeezed into the small space left, and they sipped their drinks in silence. "I've been thinking, Parksie," she started.

Parks felt apprehensive. He didn't like it when his wife started a sentence with these words.

"I've been thinking. Maybe this can work out after all. That baby. It's yours, isn't it?" She poked him with her toe. "Isn't it?"

He nodded.

"Well, I was in the shops today and I thought about it all. I've decided that I want the baby."

Parks spluttered on his whisky. "You've been at me from the beginning about getting rid of it. Now you want it?"

"Yes," she said, "I want it. It makes sense. It's the only way you can make up to me for what you did. It's the least you can do. I want her baby when it's born. You are the father, Parks. Do you understand?"

"But … but …" he was still shocked. Now this baby was something that she wanted, instead of hated?

"I need a baby," she said. "I've needed a baby for a long time. And now you've got one for me. We will get that baby, do you understand? We need a baby."

How could he not? He understood only too well how Thandi held the strings to everything. If he didn't get Busi's baby, he would be out. There would be no more job. There would be no more nice home or big TV …

"I want to see her. I want to meet this Busi." It was the first time she had spoken her name.

"You will arrange it."

Parks downed his whisky. He felt his body begin to ease. He flopped down onto the couch and pressed the remote button to activate the flat-screen TV.

"We can't force her to give us her baby."

"Your baby," said Thandi.

"How …?"

"Money talks, Parks. You should know that." She put her hand on his arm.

He didn't trust her. The next moment she could be shouting again. Her moods went up and down, faster than the Cobra roller coaster.

"She will need money. How is she going to look after the baby? Has she got family?"

"Only a mom in Jozi and an elderly granny."

"Soon she will be all alone, with a baby, while her friends are out having fun. Believe me, she will take the money and give us the child."

Parks watched *Generations* on the big-screen TV. But he couldn't concentrate. He wanted to watch the soccer, but Thandi had taken the remote and flicked the channels. It was her TV after all.

He got up and went to his room. It was meant to be a guest room, but it was the one place in the house that Thandi had let him use freely, as his office. Sometimes he would go in there just to get away from her voice.

When he opened the door, his jaw fell open and he breathed in sharply. The whole room had been rearranged. Instead of his desk there was a baby's cot, with a yellow crocheted blanket, a cupboard with baby things. Even new curtains with little yellow ducklings on.

He went over to the cot and picked up the crocheted blanket. The blood ran cold in his veins. He recognised it. It was the blanket Thandi had crocheted for her first baby, the baby she had lost. The booties were the ones that her baby's feet were meant to fill. She had kept these things all these years, unbeknown to him. He had assumed she had thrown them all out. But here they were, waiting for Busi's baby.

"It's going to be the baby's nursery." She was standing so close behind him he could smell the whisky on her breath. "I want you to paint it cream, because we don't know if it will be a boy or a girl. A cream-and-yellow colour scheme. Cheerful," she said.

He expected her to say something about keeping the baby things all these years. But she said nothing.

Parks stood silently. Memories of that fateful day had come flooding back. They were driving to the bottle store, Thandi in the passenger seat, and he was watching a young schoolgirl walking along the pavement. So sweet and beautiful, so different from his wife who was haunted by nightmares and fears. His eyes had wandered off the road. A truck had come around the corner. Thandi had screamed. There was a terrible sound of metal crunching. Thandi was lying on the road, bleeding. He had thought she was dead. But then she had lifted her head. There was lots of blood, too much blood. And at the hospital came the news that she had lost the baby and would never be able to fall pregnant again.

All these years it had sat between them like a dark shadow. Part of her had never forgiven Parks.

"Now you are going to SMS Busi and tell her where to meet you ..." she said, slurring her words. Parks's stomach tightened.

Chapter 5

Meet me at the corner at 4
2moro. Parks

And now tomorrow was today. Busi counted the hours until 4 p.m. How was she going to get through those hours? And she couldn't tell a soul about this. Not Lettie, or Asanda, or Ntombi. They would try to stop her. They would say it was suicide meeting up with him.

Deep in her heart she knew that she shouldn't do it. But how could she not? There was always a chance that he had changed his mind, that he had divorced his wife and wanted to be a father to their baby. There was always a chance …

Somehow, Busi survived the day at school. Somehow she managed to chat to Unathi about the latest spate of thefts in the school (he had lost his cell phone) without mentioning Parks. She even ignored Asisipho, the pretty, petite girl in Grade 11 who had been staring at her all through break. Was she trying to see how pregnant she was? Was she feeling sorry for her? Or was she deliberately trying to make her feel uncomfortable?

Somehow she made it back home. It was 3.30 p.m. In half an hour she would meet Parks on the corner of Freedom Avenue. She wasn't ready.

Busi started to pull clothes out of her small cupboard. It wasn't long before her bed was strewn with nearly all her jeans and tops and skirts. Nothing felt or looked right any more. Nothing fitted properly. She was beginning to panic. She had to look as good as she could for Parks. It was her pride. And that part of her that wanted him to take her in his arms again, to say those things he used to:

"You are the most beautiful girl, Busi."

"I love that little smile of yours. It makes me want to eat you up!"

Eventually she pulled on a skirt with a stretchy waistband and a low-cut top that she remembered Parks had liked. She covered it all up with her yellow winter jacket and put on her pair of high-heeled winter boots.

Busi stared at herself in the mirror on her cupboard door. Her heart was beating despite herself. Something was missing. Make-up. Busi fumbled in her drawer and pulled out her lip gloss and eyeliner and leant forward towards the mirror to apply it.

"Ooh! *Hayi!* This weather!"

The front door flew open and Busi's grandmother stumbled into the shack, shoved from behind by a blast of freezing air. Busi froze, clutching her eyeliner in one hand, her other hand moving to hide her glossy-lipped mouth.

"Oh, Busi," said her grandmother, shutting the door firmly behind her, "I don't know if I will survive this winter. It's too bad. Too bad." She turned towards her and paused, squinting in the dim light inside the shack. "You look very nice, my granddaughter," she said, moving closer.

"I'm going to Asanda's, Gogo," lied Busi. The words were out before she could stop them. Busi had promised herself that she would never lie to her grandmother again. And here she was, doing it.

"That's good, Busi. That's good," said Busi's grandmother, sitting down in the armchair. She closed her eyes and sighed.

"Before you go, make me a cup of tea. Please, Busi. I am very tired. And very cold."

Busi looked at the time on her cell phone. It was 3.50 p.m. There was just enough time, if she was quick, to make her granny some tea. She dragged a blanket from the foot of her bed and gently put it over her grandmother's knees.

"Thank you, Busi. It's good that you still do things with your friends. I'm glad for you."

Busi's grandmother was slowly sipping on her warm tea and watching the television when Busi hurried out into the cold weather. Thankfully it had stopped raining and Busi walked towards Freedom Avenue with her heart pounding in her chest.

⌘ ⌘ ⌘

Parks was early.

Busi saw his taxi coming and for a split second she considered running away, escaping him in the maze of streets. But she didn't. Instead she looked up and smiled in greeting as she reached for the door handle of the taxi. Parks was smiling down at her and Busi felt her heart tighten in her chest and her hands begin to tremble. She slid into the seat next to Parks.

"Hello, my girl," he said softly and gently. His voice washed over Busi in the way it always had, making her heart pound even faster. She clasped her hands in her lap. His voice was like the old Parks, the Parks who had cared for her, who had bought her nice things.

As the taxi pulled away, she couldn't help noticing how normal it felt to be sitting next to him like this, his profile familiar and handsome as he sat with one hand casually placed on the steering wheel. But this time he wasn't reaching across to her with his other hand to stroke her cheek, or to pull her closer. This time his other hand was on his lap. Part of her yearned for him to reach across to her like he used to do. But then she became aware of a movement behind her in the taxi.

Oh no, thought Busi, why is his *gaadjie* here? She turned around to see him. But it was not the *gaadjie*. The person in the back of the taxi, slowly moving up towards her between the row of seats, was the woman who Busi had seen before, seated in a black car, watching her. Parks's wife!

"*Haibo, kwe nze kani*?" Busi cried out in fright. Then she turned sharply to Parks, her eyes flashing. "What's she doing here?"

"It's OK," said Parks. "Just relax, Busi. She only wants to talk to you."

"Well, I don't want to talk to her," said Busi loudly, her hands beginning to fumble with the door of the taxi.

Parks drove on, still speaking calmly and quietly.

"Don't be stupid, Busi. She's not going to harm you. Just listen to what she has to say."

Busi clutched the door handle tightly in her hand as Parks swung the taxi out onto the freeway and put his foot on the accelerator. The taxi rapidly gathered speed. The tar was a grey blur through her window as the taxi went faster and faster. Even so, Busi considered opening the door and jumping. "Stop the taxi!" she cried out, "Let me out! Let me out! Stop!"

Parks drove on and Busi began to cry, her voice getting louder and louder. "Stop! Stop! If you don't let me out I'll jump! I will! I'll jump!"

"Don't be a fool," said Parks, his voice loud and firm now. His face had changed. He was no longer smiling. Instead he was frowning angrily at her. "You little fool," he said.

The nice Parks had disappeared. Now she remembered how he always was.

"Now, now, Parks. Don't scare the girl." His wife's voice was soft.

Busi's hand relaxed on the door handle and her body slumped against the car seat. She turned her face away to watch the fast-moving traffic. She couldn't look at Parks. She didn't want to risk seeing that mean expression on his face again.

Behind her she felt his wife leaning towards her. She knew that her face was very close to her right shoulder. Busi could smell her. A strange mix of perfume, alcohol and stale cooking smells. Busi leant her face against the cold glass of the taxi's window.

"Now," said Parks' wife, "you just listen to me …"

Chapter 6

Busi turned to face the woman sitting behind her in the taxi. Anger flared inside her at the sight of this woman who had Parks, who had everything she wanted. But then she saw the wife's cold, hard eyes and the anger turned to fear. This woman hated her, that was for sure. Was she going to beat her here with no one seeing?

Busi looked at Parks. Surely he would protect her. She noticed how his body had tensed up. He was gripping the steering wheel and looking straight ahead. Busi wished that he would slow down. He was weaving in and out between the cars. People were hooting.

Busi's hand moved to her stomach and she found herself talking to her baby in her head. It's all right, little baby, she said silently, it's all right. Everything is going to be all right.

"Slow down, Parks," said Busi out loud, "What do you both want with me? Just say whatever it is you want to say. And then take me home."

She was surprised to see Parks's wife trying to smile – a wide, fake smile that showed the gold star in her tooth. "Don't be frightened, Busi," she said soothingly. But her eyes still glared. "I'm sorry you are in trouble now, Busi. But you do know that you aren't anything special, don't you? My husband can't help himself." She flashed a deadly look at the silent Parks who had slowed down a little.

He didn't look at them.

"Just say what you want to say, Thandi!" he said gruffly.

Thandi turned back towards Busi. Her smile had disappeared. "The only thing special about you," she hissed, "is that you were the only one who was stupid enough to get pregnant. You are the only one who ever managed to get that right with him. Not even I succeeded in getting that right with him." She looked at him. "The accident made sure of that."

Parks winced.

Busi sat in silence. I got pregnant? she thought. I didn't get pregnant on my own. Parks said he knew what he was doing. Parks had promised her everything would be all right.

Busi opened her mouth to speak, but then closed it. She did not want to speak to this woman about Parks and condoms.

"And now you are carrying our child," said Parks's wife.

"*Our?*" Busi cried out in amazement, but Thandi cut her off.

"That child in your belly," said Thandi, pointing a long, red nail towards Busi's stomach, "is just as much his as it is yours. And what's his ... is mine." Busi recoiled from Thandi, who suddenly smiled again, that false smile that stretched her face into a grimace. "I know," continued Thandi, "that you and your granny are so poor that you can hardly afford to put food on the table."

Busi frowned and looked away.

"And I know that those parents of yours in Jozi have forgotten all about you."

"How do you know anything about my parents?" said Busi. She was shocked by what Thandi was saying.

Thandi continued, "Not even your own mother cares. Not about you. Not about your baby. Not about your grandmother."

"That's not true!" said Busi, but tears welled up in her eyes and rolled down her face.

"It *is* true!" said Thandi, her voice rising again. "It *is* true."

Busi began to sob silently and could not stop, even though she wished she could.

"Don't cry." Thandi's voice was suddenly soft and soothing again. She produced a tissue and waved it towards Busi. "Don't cry."

Thandi waited as Busi blew her nose hard and wiped her wet cheeks.

"You see, dear," said Thandi, "I am going to help you."

Busi blinked and stared at Thandi through her tears.

"Yes," said Thandi, nodding her head, "I am going to help you. You and that little baby you are carrying."

Busi blew her nose again. She noticed that Parks had turned out of the traffic, and was making his way back the way he had come. Busi hoped that she was being taken back home.

"Most wives would kill you," said Thandi, smiling again. "But not me. I am going to make sure that you and the baby have absolutely everything you need."

Busi stared at Thandi. She did not know what to say.

Thandi nodded. "Just think. I can provide lovely food and warm clothes, for you and your granny. And beautiful little baby clothes. And bottles and nappies and little baby blankets. I will get everything ready for when the baby comes. And I will make sure that you stay nice and healthy while that sweet little baby is growing inside you."

Why was this woman being so caring all of a sudden? What was she thinking? But then Busi got a picture in her mind of a little cot, with fleecy blankets and nappies all piled up neatly next to it. She knew that babies needed lots of things. Where was she going to get them?

"That is very kind," she said to Thandi. Looking out of the window she noticed, with relief, that the taxi really was driving back in the direction of her home. She wiped her cheek again, with her damp tissue.

"It *is* kind," said Thandi. "I am a very kind person. Aren't I, Parks?" she added, her voice suddenly rising.

Parks glanced briefly at his wife, and jerked his head in an unconvincing nod. Busi thought she detected a sneer on his face.

"Yes," continued Thandi, "Parks knows just how kind I am. I'm always giving him things. Everything he needs. Always tidying up the little messes he makes. Taking him back again."

Thandi's voice grew more high-pitched, and Busi clutched at the door handle. The taxi was now only a few streets from Busi's home.

"Here," said Thandi, opening her handbag and pulling out a roll of banknotes. She held it towards Busi between two long, crimson fingernails. "Take it. It's the first of much more money. Much more money for you and that baby!"

Busi put out her hand slowly. The roll of money passed from Thandi's hand to hers. Busi felt the crispness of the banknotes between her fingers. She closed her fingers around the roll and saw that they were all one-hundred-rand notes. How many were there? Ten? No, more than that. Twenty?

The taxi drew to a stop at the corner at the end of Busi's street. Parks turned to look at Busi. Busi looked at him. Suddenly it was as if Busi saw him for the first time. Really saw him. And to her he looked like a little boy. A little boy in a big man's body.

Then Busi looked back at Thandi. She was sitting quite still, eyes burning into Busi's face. Her hands were folded over her large stomach, which bulged against her soft, expensive-looking winter coat.

Thandi seemed triumphant now. "There will be more where that came from. And then, when the time comes, we will take the baby and you won't have to worry any more. I already have a room for the baby – it's beautiful. I will even let you see …"

And then Busi realised, with horror that they weren't there to help her. They were there to buy her. This leering woman was buying the baby. "Nothing is *mahala*, my child," she remembered her mother saying.

Busi was disgusted. There was no way she was going to let Parks and his wife go off with her baby, as if she, Busi, didn't exist.

But then she thought of her friends at school. If there were no baby, she could be at Asanda's house right now, planning parties, having her hair done, going out late … like old times. If she had no baby … Suddenly that wad of real money felt good as she imagined all she could buy with it. And she could work out the problem of what happened to the baby later. Right now she was cold, and hungry. After all, didn't Parks owe her?

The taxi stopped and, still clutching the money, she slid off the front seat, her feet reaching to the muddy ground. Just then she heard a call. It was Unathi, who had spotted her and was walking towards her. At once the money felt dirty in her hands. No! She could not be bought. This woman wasn't going to own her baby. She wanted nothing to do with her! In an instant she threw the banknotes back into the taxi and slammed the door behind her.

Parks started shouting, but she couldn't hear what he was saying. She started running towards Unathi.

The taxi roared off, splattering mud onto people walking by.

"*Hayi!*" a pedestrian shouted angrily.

"Busi!" Unathi's face was so open, friendly, compared to Parks and his wife. But then he saw the taxi roar past. "Busi, you're not still seeing Parks, are you?" Unathi looked shocked.

Busi looked after the taxi. She felt hollow, drained, like she had just written a difficult exam – and failed.

"Busi, wasn't that Parks's taxi?" Unathi asked.

"So what if it was?" she asked. Who was Unathi to tell her what to do?

But then she saw his hurt face. How could she say such things? It was because of the terrible regret she felt now, her hand empty when it could be filled with banknotes. She should have taken the money. Parks owed her!

Unathi turned away.

She couldn't let him go now too. "Unathi, I'm sorry …" she started saying.

But just then Asisipho came down the road, the pretty girl in the grade below. Her braids were in a neat ponytail, her skin was chocolate smooth, and she was giving Unathi a delighted smile. "Hey, Unathi. I heard you were DJ-ing at my cousin's party on the weekend. Can I give you some suggestions?"

And now he was smiling back. "Sure … Why don't you come to my house and I can show you what I've got planned?" He hesitated, looking at Busi's scowling face. "You could come too if you want, Busi."

Asisipho said nothing.

"No, it's OK. I'm not even going to the party. What do I care about the music?"

She sounded offhand, even rude. But they couldn't see that when she turned away from them to walk home, she was crying. She longed for her mother, but she knew that nobody could sort out all her problems. It wasn't like when she was little, and her mother would dry her tears and make her hot chocolate, and all her problems would disappear. Right now her problem was getting bigger by the day.

Parks was right. He was the father. She should take the money, not chase him away. And maybe he and his wife could even give the baby a better life. Maybe she was being selfish? Her mind was seething with doubts and regrets.

She got back to her shack. Her granny was asleep on her chair.

"Gogo," she said, shaking her gently.

"It's all right, Khanya, I'm coming now," she murmured.

Busi felt cold. Khanya was her mother's name. Was her granny losing her mind?

"It's me – Busi," she said. "My mother is in Joburg."

Her granny's eyes opened. "What are you telling me that for?" she said. "I know who you are." She pointed to the counter. "I got some stock and vegetables from the uncle at the spaza shop," she said. "Will you prepare them?"

But by the time the spinach and pap was ready, her granny was asleep again, and did not want to wake up. Busi ate alone, the candle throwing long shadows across the table.

After she had managed to help her grandmother to bed, she lay down herself, listening to music on her cell phone. The song's lyrics were about love. Why were songs never about being hungry or penniless or pregnant, and wondering what would happen to you? They were always about falling in love or dancing or following your dreams – things that had nothing to do with her life now.

As if the cell phone understood her irritation, it beeped with a low battery alert. She lay in the dark, hearing the cars in the distance, and shouting and laughing, as other people got on with their lives. But then her cell phone beeped again and an SMS lit up her screen with an unfamiliar number.

This isn't ova yet.

Parks's wife. That evil woman. There was no way she could let her have the baby. She pressed DELETE just before her phone went completely dead.

⌘ ⌘ ⌘

Parks and Thandi drove in silence. Silence so thick you could slice it with a knife. Only when he jumped a red robot did she hiss, "Slow down. You'll kill us."

"Let's just leave it now," Parks said. "We don't need that baby."

"We need that baby." His wife's voice was steel.

"So what do we do now?" Parks's voice was tense and loud.

"Now we wait," said Thandi. "We wait. Her life gets harder. She thinks of the money. We wait. There are still five months to go. Slowly, slowly, Parks. That's the trouble with you. You can never wait for anything. I, on the other hand, have had to wait 10 years for this. It's not going to hurt to wait a few more months ..."

Chapter 7

It was a new term, almost spring, and harder to hide her growing belly. She had failed most of her June exams, and as all her classmates were filling in application forms for tertiary institutions, or else thinking up crazy ideas for new businesses, she was wondering whether she would even be able to write her finals. When they weren't talking about exams they were talking about the Matric dance – what they were going to wear, who they were going with.

"There's no way I can go," Busi told her friends. "There's no Matric dance dress that will be able to hide this bump in two months' time."

She could tell from the half-hearted way the girls tried to persuade her to come, that they secretly agreed.

⌘　⌘　⌘

"So it's your Matric dance coming up," said her granny one afternoon.

She was surprised. "How do you know, Gogo?"

"Auntie May was here. She is making the dress for her granddaughter. Shiny, soft, red material, and lots of lace. The way she talks about it, it sounds like she's preparing for a wedding, not just a silly dance."

Busi could sense some envy in her voice.

But then her granny sighed, "Maybe it's a good thing you can't go. It's costing Auntie May. She's using her *stokvel* money, poor woman. On a silly dress!"

Her granny sat down on her chair. "Can you heat up the leftovers from last night, Busi? I'm feeling very tired." She leaned back, watching Busi at the stove. "If your mother was here, Busi, she could make you a dress for almost nothing. Remember all those lovely little dresses she made when you were little."

"Well, she's not here, is she!" said Busi sharply, and then regretted her words. She should never be impatient with her granny, the only person in the family who had stayed with her. It wasn't that she resented her granny's reminder of the things her mother had done for her as a child. It's just that it had deepened her feeling that nowadays her mother did not seem to care about her any more.

But Gogo was right – she should stop judging her mother. There must be a good reason why she hadn't yet come to Cape Town to help Busi. She would surely come soon. Perhaps her mother had sent her a message since she last checked her SMSes.

She reached for her phone, reflecting on how much time she spent waiting these days – not just for the baby to come, but for news from her mother, and from Parks. She couldn't believe how Parks had pushed himself into her thoughts again …

There were no new messages. The truth was that her phone hardly beeped at all now. Her friends had just about given up inviting her out at the weekend.

⌘ ⌘ ⌘

"Ooh, there's the new mommy!"

"Looking so healthy and big!"

Princess and her friends were at it again as she walked into school on Monday.

Busi ignored them and kept her head down, though she was tempted to turn around and run straight home to the comfort of her bed and her gogo's gentle company. It was getting harder to attend classes. She felt so tired and unmotivated. It seemed that, as her tummy got bigger, she found it more and more difficult to concentrate. As the Matric exams approached, she fell further and further behind.

"Busi, do you know the answer? Busi?"

Busi jolted in her seat.

"What?" she said, responding to her name, "Sorry, Miss, what did you say?"

"Never mind," said Miss Nombembe. "Can anyone else answer?"

After class Miss Nombembe called her in. "Busi, we talked about you at the staff meeting. You are not going to manage your finals this year. It's probably best that you keep coming to school, but you will have to register again next year. Can you ask your parent or guardian to come in and we can talk about this?"

Busi thought of her sick granny at home. "It's fine. They know."

At break time she walked across the quad to meet Unathi. He often had some tasty something for her in his lunchbox. "I'm not hungry," he would say. "It would be wasted if you don't eat it." And she would eat up the leftovers of delicious chicken stew, or strips of fried fish. Unathi and his father really knew how to cook. Sometimes it was the best meal she had all day, as her granny's pension money began to run out towards the end of the month, and they lived on very little.

But today Unathi wasn't alone. Asisipho was chatting to him, playing him a song on her cell phone. They both looked up as Busi approached. Busi saw Asisipho frown, but Unathi had his usual wide smile for her.

"Want some chicken pieces, Busi? My dad did them just the way you like."

Busi didn't want to look needy in front of this girl. "I'm not hungry," she said.

"Sounds good," said Asisipho. "Can I taste one?"

And Busi had to watch her chomp through the chicken drumstick that her own stomach was aching for.

"Thanks, Unathi." Asisipho gave him a sunny smile.

Just then her friends walked by, and she went off with them, giving a wave to Unathi as she went and ignoring Busi.

"She's got some good music," said Unathi. "I wouldn't be surprised if she was a DJ one day; she's got an ear for it."

Busi felt a rush of jealousy. "I'm also quite musical."

Unathi looked surprised. "I didn't know you were interested in music, Busi. You're not even in the choir."

Busi felt foolish. Of course she wasn't very musical; her friends even teased her about how she couldn't sing in tune.

"Well, I know what music I like," she said.

She looked over at Asisipho, now talking and laughing with her friends.

Unathi followed her gaze. "She's a nice girl," he said. "She's going through tough times. She was telling me how her mother's just lost her job."

So what, thought Busi. That was nothing compared to *her* problems. How could Unathi think that Asisipho needed his support. Anyway, Unathi was *her* rock. He couldn't be someone else's rock too. She realised how strongly she felt about him, how possessive. At the same time she knew she was being unfair. Why shouldn't he care about Asisipho?

"She seems happy enough," Busi said.

The bell rang and they started walking back to class.

"See you after school. Wait for me. Let's walk home together," Unathi said, and flashed her one of his great smiles.

She still had him, that's what that smile told her. Something in her eased.

But as she waited for Unathi after school, her heart sank to see him coming towards her with Asisipho walking alongside.

"Asisipho is coming to download some music on my hard drive at home," he told her.

He had a sheepish look on his face.

As they walked, Asisipho and Unathi chatted about various bands. "Oh, he's my favourite rapper," Asisipho said. "You like him too, Unathi? Hey, we've got the same taste."

"Do you like his music?" Unathi asked, trying to include Busi.

"Never heard of him," said Busi. And she hardly said another word all the way to her house. She knew she was being rude, but she couldn't help it.

When they got to her gate Unathi frowned at her. He was angry that she was behaving badly, she knew. But she couldn't stop herself.

She watched them walk off together. She watched to see if they would hold hands. Unathi had said they were just friends. But Busi could see that Asisipho really liked him. She could tell. It was a matter of time. Busi knew what happened when guys got girlfriends. They weren't your friend any more. The girls wouldn't let them. Anyway, girlfriends took up all their time, especially in those first months … if Unathi and Asisipho got together it would probably be just when her baby was due.

"I'll be there for you …" Unathi had promised her. It looked like that promise was about to be broken.

As she pushed the door open she heard her grandmother's hacking cough. She hadn't managed to shake it off after the winter and it was getting worse and worse. Sometimes there were flecks of blood on her handkerchief.

"Let me prepare the supper, Gogo. You relax," she said.

"There's hardly anything left," said her granny. "We will just have to have the leftovers from last night." She saw Busi's worried face. "Don't worry, child. I'm not hungry. There is enough for you. And I'm sure your mother will send something soon."

Busi could hear the tension in her granny's voice. It was too much. Busi lay on her bed and sobbed. Then she wiped her eyes and sent an SMS to her mom:

> mom we need u. wen r u comin home?

She lay down and waited for a reply. But deep down she knew her mom wouldn't come anytime soon. The light was fading outside. She could hear the sounds from the streets as people came home from work, relieved that it was the beginning of the weekend.

Then the beep of a message.

Please let this be from you, Mom, thought Busi to herself, as she sat down on her bed to read the message. *Please.*

> I need to meet u 2mor. It's
> important. Parks

She thought of his wife in the back seat of the taxi. She remembered the feeling of the money in her hand.

Busi frowned to herself and then texted back a reply:

> ok. no wife. Jst u.

Busi held her breath as she waited for his reply. She felt a wave of relief when it came.

> ok. Same place. 10am

The next morning Busi changed into the baggiest clothes that she could find, and covered herself up with her grandmother's large coat.

Her grandmother was still sleeping. She was sleeping later and later in the mornings – so unlike before, when she would be up before Busi. It certainly made it easier for Busi to sneak out without saying anything. But Busi was worried. It was like her granny was slowly slipping away. Somehow her grandmother had always managed to make sure that there was food in the house. Lately, though, she had not left the house at all to buy food. Busi knew she had to do something. She began to walk determinedly towards the corner where Parks always met her.

He wasn't late. He stopped at the curb and Busi looked into the taxi carefully before she opened the door.

"She'd better not be hiding in the back," she said firmly.

Parks shook his head.

"I'm alone," he said. "Get in."

"I don't want to go far," said Busi. "Just park along the road somewhere, OK?"

Parks shrugged and Busi got in.

Parks did as Busi had asked and stopped under some trees, away from the houses.

Busi sat with her arms folded across her chest, her body turned away from Parks. When she spoke she looked out towards the trees. Their branches almost reached the taxi window.

"OK," she said briskly, "what do you want?"

"You probably don't believe me," said Parks, the gentleness of his voice taking Busi by surprise, "but I really just want to help."

Busi turned just a little to look at Parks. He shrugged and sighed, smiling softly at her.

"It's my baby that you are carrying, and I am worried about it," he said, quickly adding, "and about you too, of course."

Busi sat in silence for a while, watching the bare branches waving in the wind. Her head was spinning and she hardly knew what she was thinking. "None of this has anything to do with your wife?" she said softly.

"No," said Parks gently, "she doesn't even know I'm here."

Busi nodded.

"Here," said Parks.

Busi looked away from his closed fist, reaching towards her. She knew what he was clutching in his hand, and she hesitated.

Thoughts of her grandmother at home filled Busi's mind. Thoughts of the empty cupboards and the cold, leaking shack. Before she could stop herself Busi opened her palm towards Parks. She looked away as she felt the roll of banknotes pressing into her hand. Tears prickled in the corners of her eyes, and she pressed her lips together and swallowed hard. "Thanks," she said softly. "Please take me home now."

The wind tossed up papers and leaves against Busi's legs as she walked the distance from the corner where Parks had dropped her off, to the closest shop. She shook her head against the wind, and lifted her chin. I'm thinking about hot samp, soft red kidney beans and a juicy piece of meat, so tender that it just falls off the bone, thought Busi to herself, already imagining herself and her grandmother tucking in.

Chapter 8

"That shirt looks perfect on you, chommie. And it hides your bump."

Asanda was right – Busi could see in the mirror. "I'll take it."

The girls were out shopping. For once Busi had a bit of money, and it felt like the old days as they all commented on the latest fashions and tried on outfits. For a few hours she stopped worrying about everything as the girls did their bargain hunting.

"Come on," said Ntombi. "You can wear that to Thabiso's tavern this weekend. Some of the Matric DJs are doing a little fundraiser for the Matric dance."

"I'm not going to the dance," said Busi.

"That doesn't mean you can't come to the party," said Asanda. "And with that shirt you'll look as gorgeous as you usually do!"

After the shopping they sat in a fast-food restaurant, sipping milkshakes with their parcels beside them.

"Unathi will be there," said Lettie, winking at Busi. "Come on, it'll be fun. You need to get out."

"Maybe," said Busi.

"Oh no," said Ntombi. "You will say yes, otherwise you can't go home. And you can't change your mind, do you understand?" She shook her finger in Busi's face as the others laughed.

"OK," Busi said. "I'll come."

⌘ ⌘ ⌘

Her granny was delighted to see her getting ready. "I haven't heard you singing for such a long time, child. It's good you're getting out now when you can."

Busi didn't want to think about what those words meant right now. "I know, Gogo. And I will make sure that someone walks me home safely – you don't need to worry."

Her granny nodded and started to say more, but then had one of her coughing fits that always frightened Busi.

"Are you all right, Gogo?" she asked. "Should I stay at home with you?"

Eventually her granny could speak. "If you stayed home every time I coughed you would be here all the time. No, get off with you and enjoy yourself!"

The girls picked her up, their faces shining with make-up and excitement. Busi used some of Parks's money to pay for her entrance ticket. She stopped herself from worrying about it. Tonight she was here to have fun!

It had been so long since she had gone out that she had forgotten how noisy these kinds of places were. The music blared, and the air was so smoky she felt as if she could hardly breathe. The others went to get cooldrinks.

"No alcohol for you," said Ntombi. "You've got to look after that baby."

Busi wished she hadn't mentioned it. She didn't even feel like drinking, and she didn't want to be reminded why she shouldn't.

Olwethu came up and took Ntombi, then Themba and Lettie started dancing.

Busi looked on. Where was Unathi? Then she saw his familiar, lanky figure on the dance floor. She smiled. His long arms and legs flew out when he danced. He looked a little like a wind-up toy. She was standing up to go to him when she saw Asisipho opposite him, dancing closer and closer, so that eventually they were just about touching. Busi sat down again. She noticed Asisipho's tight shirt, hugging her curvy body as she swayed her hips. She noticed how Asisipho didn't take her eyes of Unathi's face.

The music slowed down, and Asisipho put her arms around Unathi's neck. They rocked slowly together for a while. The beat got wilder, and they fell apart again.

Busi felt a burning inside her. She knew Asisipho liked Unathi. But was Unathi interested in Asisipho?

Someone came to sit next to her. It was Princess, wearing a tight, short skirt and a little vest with silver sequins. Her face was thick with make-up.

"Glad to see you found something to wear," said Princess. "You must have had to look in the maternity section."

Busi sighed in desperation. What was it about Princess that made her so want to hurt anyone she could?

Princess had seen her looking towards the dance floor. "Isn't it sweet to see new love blossoming?" she said.

Ntombi and Olwethu joined them, sitting down together, laughing. "What are you saying, Princess?" asked Ntombi.

"Nothing," said Princess. "Just that it's nice to see that Unathi is getting himself a girl, finally."

"What do you mean?" asked Ntombi, looking at Busi.

"Asisipho. They look so sweet together, don't they?"

They all looked at Unathi and Asisipho still dancing together. As they watched Asisipho put her hand on Unathi's shoulder. He bent down to her and she said something into his ear. He smiled and nodded.

Busi suddenly felt sick, and tired. How had she thought that Unathi would stay interested in a girl who had someone else's baby inside her?

Then she saw Unathi coming over, Asisipho following him. Did they have to come and rub it in? "I need to get some air," she said, standing up.

"Busi," started Unathi. But she brushed past him.

"Hey," he called after her, "aren't you staying for my DJ set?"

She turned back to see if he looked like he wanted her to be there. But Asisipho was touching his arm again, and he was looking down at her. Busi walked away, not noticing that he had looked up again, started to follow her, and then given up. But she turned back just in time to see Asisipho pull Unathi's face towards her to give him a kiss.

Outside in the cold air Busi felt the tears on her cheeks. What had she been thinking, coming here with all these people? This was not her life any more. And Unathi was lost to her. Unathi, who had always been there for her, was being snapped up by Asisipho. Busi had missed her chance, had lost her best friend.

She walked home quickly, ignoring the whistles from a group of drunk men at the corner. One lurched towards her and she started running, feeling frightened for the first time. She was glad she was not in high heels.

When she got home she felt sick with exhaustion. She was glad her granny was fast asleep so she didn't have to pretend that she had had a good time.

As she was undressing her phone rang. It was Lettie.

"How could you leave like that?" she shouted. "We have all been so worried, and looking for you. You didn't tell us you were going or anything. Only now Unathi told us he saw you leaving."

"I'm sorry," Busi whispered.

Lettie disconnected the call without saying goodbye.

Busi lay in bed and wept into her pillow. It had been a mistake to go to the tavern, to think that everything could be like it was before. She would not make that mistake again.

On Monday morning the chatter at school was all about the party. The girls had forgiven her for rushing away, but they stopped trying to include her in everything. She had said no too often, perhaps. None of them said anything about Unathi and Asisipho. And she was too proud to ask.

Chapter 9

Busi was deeply into her eighth month of her pregnancy. She often woke up exhausted after restless nights, but at least she didn't have to go to school. While her classmates were writing their exams, she was spending her days at home – long days when both she and her granny slept most of the time.

Usually she woke at night because the baby pressed on her bladder and made her want to go to the toilet. But one night something else woke her. Busi lay quite still in bed and blinked at the darkness. The south-easter was howling around the shack, rattling the sheets of corrugated iron that made up the walls. Busi sighed. It had just been the wind shaking the house and whipping the sand up against the window panes. She lay for a moment and then turned over, shifting her weight to make herself comfortable.

There it came again. A sound. What was that? And it was coming from inside the shack, not outside.

Busi sat up.

"Gogo?" Busi called softly into the darkness.

The sound was coming from her grandmother's bed. Busi sprang up, and frantically pushed the curtain aside. She rushed towards her grandmother's bed, switching on the light as she did so.

Busi's grandmother lay limply, the top half of her body falling off her bed. Her head was hanging down, and her breath was gurgling in her throat.

"Gogo!" screamed Busi, feeling panic rising up inside her. She tugged at her grandmother, pulling her back up onto her pillows. "Gogo!" she cried again, bending over her, and looking anxiously into her face. Her grandmothers' eyes were closed and her breath was shallow. "Gogo! No!" shouted Busi in panic. "Don't leave me!"

Busi rushed around the shack, wildly searching for her cell phone. Suddenly she could not remember where she had put it. At last she found it on the floor by her bed and began to fumble with the keys, her hands shaking. It was hard to see the numbers and she realised that tears were blurring her vision.

With a sigh of relief Busi suddenly remembered, very clearly, what had happened the last time she had visited the clinic. The clinic sister had taken her firmly by the arm and looked into her face and said, "Put this number into your cell phone. It's the emergency number for an ambulance in your area."

Busi had nodded vaguely, but the sister had waited while Busi punched the number into her phone.

The clinic sister had patted her arm, and smiled. "For a girl in your situation, it's important," she had said. "You never know when you might need it."

Busi held her breath as she searched her directory for the number, found it and dialled it.

"Come quickly," she almost shouted into her phone as she heard a voice answer. "Please! Come quickly."

⌘ ⌘ ⌘

The paramedic turned from where he stood, tending to her grandmother on her bed. "Your grandmother has had a heart attack. I'm very sorry."

Busi lifted her damp face from where she had hidden it behind her hands.

A neighbour, awakened by the arrival of the ambulance, stood with her arm around Busi's shoulder, sipping a cup of tea. She had made for Busi, but Busi hadn't taken a drop.

"Is she going to be all right?" asked Busi

softly, watching the other paramedic wheeling a stretcher in through the rickety front door.

"She is old," said the paramedic, with a slight shrug of his shoulders, "but she is stable now. She must come with us. The hospital is the best place for her now."

Busi nodded her head slowly. "Yes," she said, her voice thick with emotion. She noticed that another neighbour had begun gathering up her grandmother's possessions. Without a word they were putting together items of clothing – a hairbrush, a jar of cream, her slippers.

Busi watched her grandmother being moved from her bed to the stretcher.

"I will go with her," said the neighbour softly into Busi's ear. "It's best if you stay here for now. There is nothing more that you can do now. Try to get some sleep."

Busi nodded vaguely. And then they were gone. The night sky was tinged red by the light of the departing ambulance, and the cold wind bit into her flesh through her winter nightgown.

Another neighbour led Busi back inside. "Sleep now, Busi. There is nothing more to be done except to pray." As she left through the shack door, she looked over her shoulder. "Lock the door well, my girl," she said. "Now you are on your own."

Chapter 10

Busi lay in bed in the dark, frightened by the emptiness and silence around her. Usually she would hear her granny's soft snoring. She reached for her cell phone and sent an SMS to her mother. "Gogo has had a heart attack. You must come quickly, Mama. You must!"

Busi pressed SEND and then lay back heavily against the pillows. She imagined her mother, somewhere in Jozi, being woken by the sound of her buzzing phone. As she lay, she gently stroked her belly with one hand. She could feel no movement. The baby must be asleep, she thought.

Busi stared for a long while at her cell phone, willing an answer from her mother. None came. She fell into a deep and dreamless sleep.

⌘ ⌘ ⌘

Busi woke up with a jolt. Her heart skipped a beat. It was a beep from her cell phone that had woken her.

"Mama!" Busi studied the text message on the phone before her:

I will be there soon my daughter.

Stay strong! Do not lose hope!

Busi read the message over and over before replying:

But I am not strong Mama. You

must come. You must come.

Now.

No reply came then.

As daylight filtered through the gaps in the shack walls, Busi stood up and slowly washed herself. She tidied the whole house, stripped her grandmother's bed and washed all her linen. Then she went outside to hang up the sheets, which smacked and tugged in the wind as she pegged them on the line.

She was still outside when a message finally arrived. All it said was:

I will come

Mrs Mathabane, the neighbour who had travelled with her grandmother in the ambulance, came back later that morning.

"Your gogo is comfortable," she said. But then, clicking her tongue, she added as she walked out, "Your poor grandmother. It's you who have caused this. It's all been too much trouble for her to deal with. Too much."

Busi looked down at the floor and bit her lower lip. Shaking her head, Mrs Mathabane walked away, shutting the door firmly behind her.

Busi sat slumped in a chair all morning. Sometime in the afternoon her friends came to the door and knocked softly. Busi did not move.

"Hey, Busi!" came Lettie's voice through the door, "Open up. We heard about your granny. Hey, Busi! Open up and let us in."

Still Busi did not move.

"Hey, Busi!" This time it was Ntombi's voice. "Let us in. We are all here. We brought you something."

Busi ignored her, resting her head on the back of the armchair and closing her eyes.

"Hey, Busi!" Busi recognised Asanda's voice. "We're getting hungry and cold out here. Let us in. We're not going away until you do."

There was silence for a moment, then Asanda added, "And if we all catch cold, it will be your fault."

Busi heard a faint giggle from someone.

"Come on," said Lettie. "We're freezing out here."

With a sigh Busi stood up from the chair and moved towards the door.

"OK," she said, her voice heavy, "I'm coming."

Busi opened the door and her three friends all tumbled in. She hadn't wanted to open up, but suddenly her home seemed lighter, brighter as they all spun around her, hugging her and all talking at once. Despite herself, Busi couldn't help smiling a little.

"A cake!" said Lettie, producing a white box from under her arm. "We brought a cake."

"Shame your gogo is so sick," said Lettie with a frown. "We wanted her to have some."

"Are you alone here?" asked Ntombi. "Is your mother not back yet?"

"She's coming tomorrow," said Busi, lying. She did not want their sympathy.

Ntombi opened the box to show her the squares of chocolatey, creamy cake inside.

"You forgot my birthday," said Ntombi, pretending to be cross, and then, laughing, "but we didn't forget you!"

Asanda boiled the kettle and made tea, and the others sat down on chairs and on Busi's granny's unmade bed. Busi listened as they chattered on, telling her all about who had been getting up to what at school.

"You hear Asanda's in love?" joked Lettie. Asanda smiled and looked at the floor.

"Wow, Asanda not fighting back and denying the story? It must be true," said Busi, trying hard not to seem down.

"It's true, all right," said Ntombi. "You will have to meet him."

Busi tried to look interested. But it was a huge effort. There was only one thing now she really wanted to know.

"How's Unathi?"

The girls looked at each other. "Fine," Ntombi and Lettie said at once.

"I haven't seen him for a while. He used to bring me school notes. But since I'm not writing the exams this year I haven't seen him since that night." She took a deep breath. "Is he going out with Asisipho?"

The girls looked at each other. "I think it's more the case that Asisipho went out with him for a little bit," said Asanda, and the others laughed.

"What do you mean?" asked Busi, her heart beating faster.

"Poor Asisipho really likes Unathi," said Asanda. "And they did date a few weekends. But it's over now. I don't think Unathi's heart was really in it."

"I think Unathi's heart was broken by somebody else," said Lettie, looking at Busi.

"Someone who rushed away before he played his set at that party, and since then has been avoiding him."

"Oh, Lettie," said Busi. "Do you really think that he's still interested in me?"

"I honestly don't know," said Lettie. "You haven't been very nice to him, have you?"

"Can I put a piece of cake here for your granny?" asked Ntombi quickly – kind Ntombi, changing the subject.

"We need to go," said Lettie. "We need to go and do that revision for Geography tomorrow."

And with a flurry they left, and Busi was alone again.

She sat wondering about Unathi. Now he would only be thinking of exams, no doubt, exams that would be his passport to a whole new life next year, very different from Busi's. All of her friends – they were like birds ready to fly, ready to soar into the sky and taste freedom at last. All except Busi.

"I can't do it, Mom," Busi said into the empty silence of the shack. I can't keep going. Why don't you come?"

The baby kicked her hard and she winced, holding her stomach.

Chapter 11

Parks arrived at home to see a stranger with a red cap leaving the house.

"Who was that?" he asked Thandi.

She was sitting in the lounge, her handbag next to her, her purse open.

"No one you know. By the way, Parks, Busi is alone. Her granny's in hospital. It's a good time to get her – she will need help now. She will agree to give up the baby."

"How do you know?" Then it dawned on Parks. "You have got yourself a spy, haven't you? You are paying someone to spy on Busi for you."

"Spying, what spying?" said Thandi. "I'm just helping out someone who doesn't have much money, that's all. And if they want to tell me some neighbourhood gossip, all the better." She frowned. "Let's hope the granny dies. Then she will have to give us the baby."

Parks went to the drinks cabinet. "Well, we are not killing off her granny."

"Of course not!" said Thandi. "Would I ever think of such a thing?"

Knowing you, I wouldn't be surprised, thought Parks. He sipped his whisky.

"I've got more baby things, Parks. Beautiful things. We are going to be so happy. You'll see," said Thandi, hugging a cushion to her chest.

Parks saw the cuddly blankets, soft toys and babygros stacked on the table. He sighed. He had hoped that Thandi would get over this, but now it had become a dangerous obsession. For his own safety and peace of mind he would have to get hold of that damn baby.

Thandi stood up, took his whisky glass from him and put it down. "Come. We are paying Busi a visit."

⌘ ⌘ ⌘

Busi woke with a jolt. Someone was banging on the door. Sleepily Busi stumbled to open it, thinking that one of her friends had probably forgotten something.

"What have you left …?" she mumbled as she opened it.

But it was not her friends. Before she had a chance to slam the door shut, Parks and his large wife had pushed her back into the shack.

"Get out!" shouted Busi as she stumbled backwards. Parks's strong hand steadied her.

"You have no right ..." she said loudly, turning to face them. "I'll call the police ... I'll ..."

"Quiet now," said Parks gently, touching her softly on the cheek. "We're not going to harm you."

"Just listen!" said Parks's wife.

Busi turned away from them, covering her ears with her hands.

"No," she said, "I won't listen to you!"

"Be quiet!" Busi heard Parks say to his wife, "Let me do the talking!"

His wife opened her mouth to say something, looked at Busi, then closed it again. She nodded at Parks.

Busi felt Parks moving closer to her. She felt him putting his arm around her shoulders.

"We heard about your grandmother," he said, leaning down and speaking so softly that Busi could feel his breath close to her ear. She closed her eyes and breathed deeply.

Oh, Parks, she thought, I loved you so much. He was so close to her that she could smell the familiar scent of his aftershave. A part of her wanted him to envelop her in his arms.

"Everything is going to be OK," she heard him say. "Let me take care of everything. Let me take care of you. Let me take care of the baby. *My* baby. Give it to us. Give it to me. We will be able to give it everything it could want in life. Everything. When the baby is born you must give it to us. We will give it a wonderful life. We have money, and no children of our own. We can do it. You must let us."

Busi's eyes flew open, and she pulled away. Then she turned to face him, her fists clenched at her sides, her eyes flashing. "'*My* baby'!" she said, her voice rising. "Did you say '*my* baby'?" Busi's heart was beating furiously in her chest. She rushed to the door of the shack and flung it wide. "*Get out!*" she screamed, waving her hands wildly. "Get out of my house! Get out of my life! I will never ..."

Busi paused to catch her breath. Her mind was in turmoil. Parks was staring at her, open-mouthed. His wife was behind him, pushing him forward. Busi was aware that she was shouting loudly, and that she had picked up a frying pan from the stove and was waving it in their direction. Suddenly she felt the baby kick fiercely, and she clutched at her stomach with her other hand.

"Calm down!" said Parks, "Our baby ..." and he moved towards her.

"It's *my* baby!" shrieked Busi, aware that she was frightening Parks. "*My* baby! Not yours! Now go! Go! Go now!"

Parks's wife came towards her.

"Leave it …" Parks said to his wife, hustling her to the door. "This is not the right time."

Parks's wife looked at Busi, who was still waving the frying pan as if she was about to bring it down on them.

"You will regret this," Thandi said quietly. "Has anyone told you what it is really like, having a baby? Clearly not. They can cry all night; they can drive you crazy. And you are just a girl. What makes you think you will cope? Listen. That baby belongs to us, just as much as it belongs to you. We will know when the baby is born and we will be there waiting. And you, my girl, you *will* give it to us."

And then they were gone.

Chapter 12

It was early morning, still dark, when Busi stirred in her sleep. In those moments before she was properly awake, she forgot that her gogo was not soundly sleeping in the bed on the other side of her curtain. She forgot that it was a weekday, and that she had not been to school for some time. She forgot about Parks, and she forgot about his wife. In those few precious seconds she even forgot about the baby inside her, almost ready to be born.

But then, as the roof creaked, and the metal walls of the shack shuddered, Busi opened her eyes and remembered everything. She lay still and alone beneath her blankets. She knew that there was no longer any milk or tea or coffee. She knew that there was only one cupful of mealie-meal left, and a dry crust of bread.

Busi sighed and rolled over. Maybe I will lie here for just a little longer, she thought to herself, closing her eyes and willing herself back into a deep sleep. She drifted off and dreamt of her childhood, when she was still happy and innocent, living with her mother, father and Gogo.

In the dream she was helping her mother with chores in the house. She was just old enough to boil the kettle by herself and she had made her mother a cup of tea. Her mother had forgotten to drink it. Not wanting it to go to waste, Busi picked up the mug and carried it to her mother in the yard, where she was hanging washing. But she tripped on a stone, spilling tea all over the clean sheets on the line. "Oh dear," she was saying to herself in her dream, "Everything is wet, Mama. Everything."

Busi sat up. The dream was over, but the dampness remained. Confused, she pulled back the sheets and blankets. She looked down at herself in alarm, jumping out of her bed and feeling the bottom sheet with her hand. Her wet pyjamas clung to her legs. Her sheet was wet to the touch.

Busi's hand moved up to her mouth. "It can't be," she said aloud, racking her brain to remember everything the clinic sister had said to her. She looked up at the shelf next to her bed and rummaged through the books, pushing aside her school books to find the booklets and pamphlets she had been given at the clinic.

Finding a small booklet called *You and your baby*, she sat down again on her wet bed and paged through it quickly. At last she found the relevant section: "When your waters break it means that your baby will soon be born. You must immediately get help because your baby is no longer protected in the womb, and it must be born, by whichever means possible."

Busi sat still for a moment. She felt stunned as she read the final line over and over: "… and it must be born, by whichever means possible."

Suddenly she sprang into action. She needed to get to hospital urgently. Now! She grabbed her phone. She didn't know what exam was being written, but surely one of her friends would be able to help her. She would have to send a PLEASE CALL ME – she had no airtime. But her phone screen was blank. Of course. She hadn't been able to charge it.

"Oh no," she groaned. Should she go around to Lettie's house close by? But what if Lettie wasn't there? No. She must get straight to hospital. She dressed herself as quickly as she could, pulling on loose clothing, and noting that her "waters" seemed to have stopped flowing.

Busi locked her front door behind her and, clutching a small bag she had packed as a precaution a few weeks before, she began to walk quickly towards the taxi rank. She did not notice a neighbour in a red cap open her front door, watch her closely, and then close the door again.

Busi climbed aboard a taxi that was going towards the hospital. She breathed a sigh of relief as she paid the taxi fare. It was the last of the money from Parks. She thought about the return fare and calculated that the few coins remaining in her purse might just cover it.

The taxi seemed to take forever to get to the hospital. Every road on the route to the hospital seemed to be clogged with traffic. Busi leant back against the seat and took a deep breath. She felt anxiety mounting inside her, but she remembered how important it was to stay calm. Whatever happened, Parks and his wife should not know that her baby was about to be born. In her mind she imagined her baby nestling in Thandi's arms, her red nails stroking its cheek while Parks looked on, smiling. No, thought Busi to herself, that could not happen! Not at any cost! She would have to give a false name at the hospital so that they could not trace her.

Eventually the taxi drew to a halt outside the hospital, and Busi stood up and made her way slowly to the exit. She climbed down onto the pavement and looked towards the hospital entrance. Strangely it seemed very far away, although she knew it was just an easy stroll.

She took a step forward, clutching her bag against her stomach. Oh, Mama, she thought in panic, where are you? She took another step, and then another. The security guard seated at the entrance looked up at her as she approached, then stood and moved towards her as an agonising pain gripped her tummy. She cried out, feeling her legs buckling beneath her, "Help me! My baby ... my baby is coming!"

Chapter 13

Busi tried to stay calm as two nurses came running towards her, pushing a wheelchair. They positioned it next to her and hauled her up into it. Busi held onto her bag with one hand and onto the armrest with the other as the nurses pushed her towards the hospital reception at breakneck speed.

"Name!"

An overweight man in a white shirt stood over Busi with a clipboard. When she did not immediately reply he bent down and shouted into Busi's face.

"Name!"

"Thandi Mbethe," said Busi.

It was the first name that popped into Busi's mind. Thandi and Parks. Their faces swam before Busi for a second, then she forgot everything as she was gripped, yet again, by excruciating pain.

The orderly asked Busi some more questions between the contractions, and she lied in her answers to every single one. No one must know I am here, was all she could think, no one. Fear gripped her as tightly as the contractions that seized her body. Parks and Thandi must not know that I am here. They mustn't know. *They mustn't know.*

The same nurses who had wheeled her into the hospital instructed her to remove her clothes and get into a hospital robe. Then they assisted her rather roughly onto a hospital bed and wheeled her into a ward. She was vaguely conscious that there were other women there. Some of them were screaming.

Busi clutched at the sheets and called out to a passing nurse. "Help me," she cried out pathetically. "I can't do this! I don't want to do this!"

The nurse stopped for a second and cast a disinterested eye over Busi.

"Well, my girl," the nurse said coldly, tapping Busi's thigh with the cold palm of her hand, "you have no choice in the matter. You had lots of fun putting that baby in there, didn't you? Well, as you are finding out, it's not so much fun getting it out. Is it?"

Busi cried out in pain, and reached out for the nurse's hand. "Stay with me," she begged, "Please stay with me."

The nurse pushed Busi's hand away. "What are you thinking?" she said coldly. "That I have only you to attend to? You still have a long way to go. Get on with it." And with that the nurse walked off.

Busi lay back against the pillow, and took a few deep breaths. For the moment the pains had passed.

"Oh, Mama," said Busi softly, beginning to cry, "why didn't you come? Why didn't you come? Oh, Gogo, why did you leave me?"

The tears rolled down Busi's cheeks as she prepared herself for the overwhelming contractions that she knew would come again soon. And when they did, one after the other, in a seemingly endless cycle of pain, she cried out and sobbed. There was nobody there to comfort her.

⌘ ⌘ ⌘

Busi's baby was born later that day. She sighed with relief and exhaustion as she heard the doctor say, "It's a girl," and then she reached out her arms to receive her new baby.

Busi looked down at the little being cradled in her arms. She was tiny and wrinkled with a lot of black hair plastered against her head. It would take a while to sink in that this little child was now hers. The baby's eyes opened and

Busi stared deeply into the dark black pools. New life. She felt a rush of love and wonder.

A nurse urged her to begin feeding and Busi put the baby to her breast, like she had seen so many women do. The baby nuzzled, and then latched onto her nipple and sucked.

"No problem with feeding this one," said the nurse, and moved on to the next woman.

Busi's daughter drank her fill and then the nurse took her back to the nursery. Without her warm presence, Busi suddenly felt flickers of fear and loneliness again. Where was her grandmother? Where was her mother? She wanted to show them her baby. She began to cry, but even crying felt like too much effort. She sank into a deep sleep.

When Busi woke up she was gripped by a fear that her baby was gone. She sat up with a start and cried out, "Where is she? Where is my baby?"

"*Thula wena*," said a nurse, who was busy with another patient in a bed across from Busi. "She's in the nursery. Be quiet or you'll wake everybody."

"I want her," said Busi, sitting up and swinging her legs to the floor.

"You stay where you are," said the nurse, frowning. "You'll get her later when it's time to breastfeed. It's nearly supper time for you. Eat first."

Busi lifted her legs back onto the white sheets, and told herself to be calm. But her eyes looked wildly around the ward, as if Parks and his wife might appear at any moment.

Her stomach growled and she realised how hungry she was. She had not eaten for nearly two days. The smell of food that wafted down the shiny, tiled hospital passageways into the ward made her mouth water.

Busi ate every morsel of the stew that was put in front of her. She was so ravenous that she didn't mind the fatty bits of meat. It seemed to her that no food had ever tasted so good. When she was finished she pushed her tray away and slid her bare feet down onto the cold tiles.

"I'm ready to see my baby now," she said to the nurse who was handing out the food. "Where is she?"

"In a minute, in a minute," said the nurse, and then, seeing that Busi was very determined, she called out to another nurse, "*Hayi*, this child wants her child. Bring it to her please."

Busi stood in the middle of the room. She clutched her hospital robe around her. Already she was feeling stronger. She looked around the ward. There was a little cupboard next to her bed. She walked slowly towards it and opened it. Inside were her clothes and her bag containing a few things for the baby. She unzipped it, lifting out the clothes her gogo had given to her. She had not shown any interest in them at the time; she had not even asked where they came from. They weren't new. And anyway she had not wanted to look at anything to do with the baby.

Now she lay the little babygro on the hospital bed and stroked it gently. There was also a thin baby blanket and two nappies. So little, thought Busi to herself, so little with which to begin life. She had always thought that her mother would be there when the baby came, and that she would provide for them. What a fool I was, she thought.

She looked up to see a nurse bringing her little baby girl to her. She reached out and took her, gently. Then, holding her tightly in her arms, she bowed her head to kiss her daughter's little wrinkled face. The baby began to whimper and Busi lifted her to her breast and started feeding her, closing her eyes as she did so. Lost in the present moment, she forgot about everything else.

Chapter 14

Busi changed the baby's nappy and carefully dressed her in the tiny babygro. Then she kissed her sweet-smelling head and lay down with her again. She cuddled her for the rest of the evening. When the nurse came to take her back to the nursery, Busi wouldn't let her go.

"She's my baby and she stays with me," Busi said fiercely whenever a nurse came near her.

Mostly the nurses were too busy to bother with her. "Just make sure she doesn't make a noise and disturb the others," was the response from most of them.

For most of the night Busi lay with her baby girl nestled in her arms. She couldn't stop staring at her, examining her tiny fingers and her tiny toes. It was a strange mixture of emotion she felt. She was overcome with love, but at the same time she had never felt such responsibility, and it frightened her. Her head swam with thoughts about what she should do. It was like she kept going down the same dead-end street and could not find an answer.

As she lay there cuddling her daughter, a long-forgotten memory surfaced. Years ago a social worker had come to her school. She had been there to speak about teenage pregnancy. Thinking back, Busi thought how foolish she and her friends had been, wolf-whistling and giggling every time the lady had tried to talk to them about sex and pregnancy. Still, Busi had tried to listen, even though the boys in particular had been making so much noise. "Always use condoms," the social worker had said. Busi remembered how she had wanted Parks to use condoms. Why on earth had she believed him when he had said she shouldn't worry – that everything would be all right?

Busi ran her finger over her baby girl's black hair. "How sweet you are, my daughter," Busi whispered to her. "I will never let that woman have you. Never."

Busi closed her eyes and must have dropped off because she saw Thandi's face before her. She was looking straight at Busi and smiling – a horrible, sneering smile.

"You see," said Thandi to Busi in the dream, "I always said that what was his was also mine." And then Thandi turned her gaze away from Busi, to something she was holding in her arms. In her dream Busi followed her gaze and saw what it was that Thandi was looking at. It was her baby girl! Thandi's red fingernails were stroking the baby's cheek, leaving scratch marks.

Thandi looked at Busi again, pulling her lips back in a grim sneer as she said, "You see, she is mine now …"

Busi woke up with a start. "Oh, my baby girl," she whispered close to her baby's ear, "what am I going to do?"

Busi thought of her empty shack, with its empty shelves. And then she thought of her gogo, lying somewhere in this same hospital. She was certain she would never see her again. She was dying, Busi knew it.

"Gogo can't help me now, baby girl," whispered Busi, the tears streaming down her face and onto her baby. "She can't help me now."

Busi could barely bring herself to think of her mother and father. She could hardly picture their faces any more, they had been gone for such a long time.

"I love you, little girl," whispered Busi again, her tears still flowing freely, "but there is no one to help us. No one at all. Forgive me. I'm sorry. I'm sorry."

The baby yawned, and stretched, and shut her eyes. Soon she was fast asleep. She knew nothing of the world and its hardship.

Busi could not stop her tears. Then she remembered something else that the social worker had said to them that day. She had told them about something mothers could do if they could not look after their babies for any reason. It was a way to keep their babies safe from harm. Lying there in the darkened ward, Busi made a decision.

Pulling the hospital blanket up to her chin and moving slowly and quietly so as not to attract attention, she slipped out of her hospital gown and pulled on her clothes. She decided to keep the warm blanket that her baby was wrapped in, promising to return it some day.

Then, waiting until she could see no nurse around, Busi got out of her bed, leaving a pillow plumped-up beneath the bedclothes. She clutched her sleeping baby close to her chest and walked very quietly to the entrance of the ward. Far down the passage she could hear voices but, for the moment, there was no nurse in sight.

Busi dashed across the passage and down a flight of stairs. She opened her gogo's large coat and pulled it around the sleeping bundle in her arms. Busi walked quickly. She had no idea where she was, but soon she saw signs pointing to the entrance of the hospital, and she followed them.

It was now nearly 5 a.m. Busi knew exactly what she was going to do. She managed to slip past the dozing men on duty at the hospital entrance and then she was outside, in the cold and dark of the early morning.

Out on the street taxis were already picking up commuters on their way to work. Busi was relieved to find that her remaining money was still in her purse in the pocket of her coat. She hailed a taxi and was grateful when one stopped and she could clamber into the cosy warmth inside.

The *gaadjie* sucked air in through his teeth and whistled low when he saw Busi's small baby held fast against her breast.

"Where to, Sisi?" he asked gently, looking at her kindly. Busi looked at him gratefully as she told him.

"Keep your money," he said, taking Busi by surprise. "Let her have her first ride for free."

Busi bowed her head in gratitude and sat down. She looked out at the dark streets and blinked back the tears. I must be strong now, thought Busi to herself. Now is not the time for tears. I have to do this for you, my darling daughter.

And then the taxi swerved out into the main stream of traffic. Busi did not look back.

Chapter 15

Busi looked out at the dark road. Her baby lay fast asleep on her lap, wrapped in her blanket inside Gogo's coat. She shut her eyes and cast her mind back to the social worker's visit to her school when she had shown them a DVD about something called a "Baby Safe". Busi could remember it all very clearly, although at the time she could never, in a million years, have guessed that one day she would be in the same predicament.

Busi turned to the *gaadjie*. "Do you have a piece of paper?" she asked, glancing around at the other passengers in the taxi and adding, "and a pen?"

The *gaadjie* shrugged and shook his head, but a woman seated across the way from Busi took a notebook out of her bag, and tore out a couple of pages. She handed them to Busi, together with a pen.

"*Enkosi*," said Busi, and she sat with them clutched in her hand.

She stared out of the window at the passing cars.

"You better use the pen quickly," said the woman, shifting in her seat. "It's not long before I get out."

Busi nodded and looked down. Slowly, she began to write:

This is my baby. She was born yesterday. I am not able to keep her.

Please look after her for me. Please keep her safe. Please tell her that she has a mother who did not want to leave her. I could find no other way.

Thank you.

Tears splashed onto the page in front of her. Busi was grateful for the darkness inside the taxi, and she looked away, out of the window. She was still clutching the pen when the woman stood up and asked for it.

"Sorry," said Busi, suddenly startled, and handed her the pen. "Thank you."

⌘ ⌘ ⌘

Busi knew where the church was. She had even been there once, years ago. Before her parents left Cape Town Busi had been part of a church youth group. They had visited another group of children at that church. When the social worker showed the DVD at her school she had exclaimed, "Hey, I know that place! It's called St Saviour's Church!"

Busi closed her eyes and remembered for a moment how young and carefree she had been then. They had been given hotdogs and cooldrinks, and they had played games and had so much fun. She sighed deeply.

The taxi was nearly there. Busi felt a lump rising in her throat and her hands grew clammy. "Not far to go now, little one," she whispered softly to the baby, still asleep in her arms.

For the first time Busi suddenly considered the possibility that the "Baby Safe" may no longer exist. She felt her heart constrict in her chest. "Please, God," she said aloud, "please let it still be there."

Busi remembered that in the DVD the "Baby Safe" was set into a wall of the church. It was like a large, silver drawer that could be opened. When it was opened a person could put the baby into the drawer and then shut the drawer again. The DVD had stated that the drawer was heated, so that the baby would be warm, and it was also ventilated, so the baby would be able to breathe well. The DVD had also said, very clearly, that the drawer activated some kind of alarm, and as a result someone would come, very quickly, to fetch the baby. They would take it away to safety, and they would look after it and give it everything it needed.

Busi stared anxiously out of the window, waiting for the church to come into view.

⌘ ⌘ ⌘

"She must have had the baby by now!" Thandi gabbled as Parks came into kitchen. "I tell you, it's all happening, Parks. I've just got a message that she went off yesterday, early in the morning, and didn't come back last night. What else can that mean?"

When he didn't respond she went up to him and shook him. "Did you hear me? We're getting our baby today!"

"OK, OK, Thandi," he said. "But we don't even know where she is."

"We're going to find her." Thandi took away the coffee cup he had removed from the cupboard. "No time for coffee now, Parksie. We need to go."

She revved the car as Parks pulled on his jacket and they sped off. "Careful," said Parks nervously, as they narrowly missed a dog on the side of the road. Thandi kept her foot down flat on the accelerator, jumping red traffic lights and stop streets until they reached the local hospital.

"We're looking for a girl called Busi – she's my niece. She's just had her baby and we've got lots of things for her. We must see her urgently!" Thandi shouted to the receptionist.

Parks groaned inwardly. They were just going to draw attention to themselves if Thandi behaved like it was a matter of life and death.

Unperturbed, the receptionist searched her list for what seemed like ages and then looked at them. "No Busi here."

"She must be!" said Thandi in frustration. "She can't be anywhere else." She turned to Parks. "Where do you think …" But then she turned back to the receptionist, a pleased look on her face. "She is scared of her parents – maybe she gave a different name. I know she came in yesterday, so she must be here still."

"The only young girl who came in yesterday was a girl called Thandi Mbethe," said the receptionist.

"Thandi Mbethe – that's my–" spluttered Thandi.

Parks squeezed her hand. "That's who we are looking for," he said smoothly. "Where is she, please?"

"She's in Ward 24," said the receptionist. "But you can't go there now. It's not visiting hours or anything. Hey!" she called after them, but Thandi had already rushed off, followed by Parks.

They darted down the passages, bumping into wheelchairs and stretchers and startling nurses who were unable to stop them. Breathless, Thandi pushed open the door to Ward 24. They scanned the beds.

"What are you doing here?" a nurse asked.

"Where's Busi – I mean Thandi Mbethe?" asked Parks.

The nurse shrugged. "She left early this morning without even telling us. She's gone."

"No-o-o-o!" Thandi wailed.

"Come on," said Parks, pulling his wife away from the nurse who was looking at her suspiciously. "She can't be far. We'll find her."

Back in the car Thandi's face looked severe. "It's now or never. This is the last chance – for me, and for you, Parks."

Parks's mouth was dry with fear.

Chapter 16

The taxi swung into the dark street near the church, its headlights flashing across the high brick walls of the church building. Busi moved across the seats as the taxi stopped. Her feet reached for the pavement, and she felt the firm hand of the *gaadjie* on her arm as her feet touched the cold grey tar.

Looking back, she saw a frown of concern on the *gaadjie's* face. "*Enkosi*," she said absently, and turned to face the church as she heard the door slide shut.

The taxi pulled away.

Busi quickly crossed the tarred parking lot in front of the church, heading for a clump of trees and shrubs growing to one side. She stepped under the dark shelter of the trees and looked towards the building.

The entrance was floodlit by large lights. Busi blinked and then looked down at her sleeping baby. She snuggled her closer.

In the wall on one side of the entrance Busi could see a large rectangle of silver metal. The "Baby Safe". She breathed a sigh of relief. There it was. She stepped a little closer. She could feel her heart beating faster in her breast. She looked down at her baby once again. The little girl was beginning to stir. Busi felt a prickling sensation in her breasts and an instant later felt the front of her shirt wet with milk. Her baby stirred again and made a low, whimpering sound.

Busi began to walk. "Do it now," she said to herself, stepping out from the shelter of the trees. "Come on, Busi."

Busi continued to speak gently to herself as she crossed the damp, dark green lawn in front of the church building. She glanced over her shoulder, suddenly imagining that Parks and his wife were pulling up in the car park in their black car. There was no one there. The street was deserted.

In five long strides Busi found herself in front of the wide silver drawer set into the wall. She reached out with one hand and wrapped her fingers around the silver handle on the drawer. It was hard and icy cold.

Busi looked up and read the instructions printed on a square of silver metal set into the wall above the safe.

> Press the green button to open
> the safe. The safe will open.
> Place the baby into the safe. Shut
> the door. When it is sealed the
> red light will show.

Busi pressed the green button. She felt the safe unlock as she pulled on the handle, and the drawer began to open.

Carefully she shifted her baby in her arms. The drawer yawned open. She peered inside. It was padded and she could feel warmth coming from it. Busi looked down at her baby and the little girl opened her eyes and looked up at her. It was too much to bear. Through her tears the baby's face blurred until she could hardly see her any more. Slowly, gently, Busi moved her baby out from under her coat. Her hands were trembling so badly that she was afraid she might drop the baby as she lifted her up towards the safe.

A pain like no other she had ever felt before was tearing, searing, burning in her chest. For a moment it felt to her as if she would fall to the ground. She cried out, but then bit her lip to silence herself.

Busi lowered her baby into the safe and as she touched her for the last time, sobs began to rack her body. She placed the letter, crumpled now and stained with tears, on top of the bundled blanket. Then she looked away, and, placing both hands on the safe handle, Busi slowly shut the safe. Instantly the red light went on.

Busi turned from the safe and ran.

She crossed the damp lawn again, and stumbled back in amongst the trees and shrubs on the edge of the church yard. She fought her way through the vegetation until she found a protected place near the church wall, behind a tree with low, hanging branches. She sank down onto the moist soft soil and fallen leaves, pressing her hands to her mouth to stifle uncontrollable gasps of grief.

⌘ ⌘ ⌘

It was the longest three minutes of Busi's life.

"Where are they?" she said aloud to herself, "Why doesn't anyone come?"

Panic surged inside her. What if her baby remained sealed in the safe and nobody came? What if she could not get her out again? What if she was hungry and began to cry?

Busi was just beginning to move out again from behind the tree when she saw a small red car swinging around the corner. Its headlights flashed along the church wall as it turned, very quickly, into the church parking lot.

Busi hid behind the tree again.

The door on the passenger's side of the car opened, flooding the interior of the car with light so that Busi could see two people inside. A woman leapt out and ran towards the church building, carrying a large bag in one hand. A man slammed the driver's door and ran after her. The woman with the bag reached the church door first. Busi could hear their voices as they quickly unlocked the large door, and went inside.

"Yes, it has been activated," she heard the woman say. "It looks like there's a baby inside."

And then both of them disappeared inside the church building.

Busi stayed hidden amongst the plants and trees in the far corner of the church yard as she watched the sky turn pink and orange with the arrival of dawn.

She remained still, and waited.

Eventually she heard the door open, and both the man and the woman came out. They walked closely together, the man carrying the bag and the woman carrying Busi's baby, now warmly wrapped up in a large pink blanket.

Busi pushed her face up against the hard bark of the tree trunk, feeling its roughness. Every part of her wanted to cry out to them;

her whole being wanted to run out from behind the tree and take her baby from them.

But Busi did not move. Her breath came out in short, sharp sobs, and she pressed her fist into her mouth so that she would not be heard.

The woman climbed into the car and Busi could see her bending over her baby and cuddling her close.

The man opened his door, and then paused as he looked around the church grounds. "I don't think she is far away," he said aloud, before he climbed into the car. "This must have been the hardest thing for her to do. I hope she knows that her baby is totally safe with us. I wish there was a way to let her know that we will care for her child in the very best way that we can."

And then he got into the car, closed the door, and drove away.

Busi sank to her knees. She buried her face in the soft, damp leaves and clutched handfuls of the dark soil. The sky was light when she slowly stood up again. Unseen, she climbed out from among the shrubs, and, unseen, she stumbled back into the street, now busy with morning traffic. Her face was muddy and tear-stained, and her swollen breasts ached.

Chapter 17

Busi kept walking for a long time, her eyes fixed on the pavement. Eventually she reached a shopping mall where she found a taxi going in the direction of her home.

Busi fumbled in the pocket of her coat and found a collection of coins. It was enough to pay for her fare.

"*Hayi xeko!*" said a woman to Busi as she squeezed in next to her in the taxi. The woman clicked her tongue.

Busi looked down at her hands. She saw now that they were covered in dirt, grass and dried mud. Pieces of twigs and dried leaves were stuck in her braids, and she absent-mindedly pulled at them.

Busi sighed and looked down into her lap. Her gogo's yellow winter coat was covered in mud stains.

I suppose they think I've been drinking, or sleeping in the bushes, getting up to no good, thought Busi to herself.

She didn't care. She sat slumped in her seat, holding her bag loosely on her lap. Her body felt battered, and her breasts still felt full and uncomfortable. How strange to feel her arms so empty. They had never before felt so empty, so light.

When the taxi came to a stop in her neighbourhood Busi stepped down onto the street. She looked around for a moment to make sure there was nobody around that she knew and then she began to walk in the direction of her house.

She was concentrating on putting one foot in front of the other, her head down, watching her feet move from under her – heel toe, heel toe – when suddenly she became aware of a vehicle moving slowly alongside her in the street.

Busi turned her head to one side, and blinked at it from behind her dangling braids. It was Parks's wife's car! Thandi was in the driver's seat, with the window down.

Instantly Busi began to walk faster. Parks was in the passenger seat. As the car got closer to her he leaned across the driver's seat and started shouting through the open window.

"You've had the baby!" he yelled. "You've had the baby, haven't you? We went to the hospital. Where is it?"

Busi gathered all the strength she had left and, trailing her bag from one hand, she began to run as fast as she could.

Behind her she heard the car accelerate.

"What have you done with our baby?" she heard Thandi's voice screaming after her.

⌘ ⌘ ⌘

Busi ducked down an alleyway and ran between the houses, turning down narrow streets and running deeper and deeper into a maze of small lanes until she could no longer hear Parks.

She stopped for a moment and leant, panting, behind an outside toilet in someone's yard. She looked around then, unsure of where she was.

"Busi! What are you doing here?"

Busi looked around quickly and searched, with relief, for the familiar voice.

"Unathi!" she said, turning towards him as he walked towards her, smiling. It was not the first time he had appeared just when she needed him the most. "Unathi," she said again, watching his expression change as he became aware of her dishevelled appearance, "you've got to help me."

"Come," said Unathi.

Busi realised then that it was still early, and Unathi must be on his way to school. Maybe he even had an exam to write. But Unathi didn't hesitate for a moment.

"Come with me, Busi," he said, placing a reassuring arm around her shoulder. "Come, this way." Unathi led Busi quickly to his house and opened the door for her.

"It's OK," he said, "my dad has already left for work. There's no one here."

Unathi closed and locked the door behind them, and then took Busi's arm and led her to an armchair. Busi sank down into it and closed her eyes.

Unathi took a bottle of Coke from the fridge, poured Busi a large glass and gave it to her. "Drink this," he urged her as he pushed it into her hand. "You look like you could do with some sugar."

Busi sipped the Coke slowly and gratefully, feeling a little strength returning to her body.

"Tell me what's happened," said Unathi after a moment. Then he paused, and looked at Busi carefully. "You've had the baby, haven't you?" He couldn't be sure, as Busi was still wearing her gogo's large coat.

Busi sat in the chair, her body slumped. She sipped and nodded slightly.

"But where is the baby now?" asked Unathi, alarmed. "What have you done, Busi?"

"Don't you need to get to school?" answered Busi. Her voice was tired.

"Never mind that," said Unathi, coming to kneel beside Busi, and looking anxiously into her face. Perhaps he did love her still.

"Where is your baby, Busi?" he asked again.

"Safe," said Busi. She looked intently into Unathi's face. Then, after a long pause, knowing that she could trust him, she added, "But Parks is out there, Unathi. And he's angry. He's after me, Unathi. Him and his wife, they want the baby. They want to take the baby away from me." Busi began to cry softly.

Unathi sat on the armrest of Busi's chair and put his arm around her. He patted her shoulder to comfort her. "It's OK, Busi," he said softly.

She had imagined Unathi's arms around her in the last few months, but not like this – not when she felt so tired, so utterly spent.

"Listen, Busi," he said, "I will go to your house alone, and see if Parks is anywhere around. I'll get you some things if you like." He brushed some leaves off her back. "You must stay here. Then you can rest, have a bath, and I'll make you something to eat."

He stood up and looked down at her. "But, Busi, you need to tell me what you have done with your baby. You haven't done anything silly, have you?"

"No, no, Unathi," said Busi. "I promise you she is safe." But she couldn't tell him yet what she had done. Had she just made the biggest mistake of her life, giving her baby away to strangers?

Chapter 18

"We've lost her!" Thandi shrieked. "You stupid fool, we've lost her!" Parks did not point out that she was the one driving.

"Calm down, Thandi," he said. "I tell you what. Let me take you back home. She is more likely to give the baby to me. I can still get her to listen. She still ..." but he stopped. If he told Thandi that he knew Busi still had feelings for him, she would fly off the handle.

Thandi opened her mouth to say something.

"Remember, Thandi," said Parks, "you have everything. She has nothing. She won't want to give it to you. But she may give it to me."

Thandi sat silently for a moment, hands on the steering wheel. Her painted nails were chipped where she had picked off the varnish.

"All right," she said, "take me home. But come back here quickly to get my baby!" She began to cry and moved across to the passenger seat so that Parks could get in on the driver's side.

Parks breathed a sigh of relief. Thandi was dangerous in her rages, but once she started crying the danger was over, and she would listen to what Parks said.

He drove home at speed, enjoying a sense of control now that he was behind the steering wheel. When he reached the house, he stopped at the garden gate and Thandi got out, still sniffing and dabbing her eyes. He parked Thandi's car in the garage and got into his taxi. As he pulled out into the street he watched her letting herself into the house.

What he was about to do felt impossible. Why had Busi been alone? Where was the child? What had she done with it? And even if assuming Busi told him where it was and agreed to give it up, was it worth it? He wasn't sure if he even wanted a baby in the house. It was bad enough being responsible for a dog, let alone a baby. How would Thandi cope with the sleepless nights? She was volatile as it was. And she wasn't young any more. She would still want her beauty sleep and he would have to do night duty. One thing was for sure: Thandi would order him around even more than she already did.

At the same time he knew that his life would be over if he did not come home with the baby.

He was about to drive off when he heard Thandi's voice. "Wait!" she shouted. She was running down the garden path holding a yellow crocheted blanket. "Take this, to wrap our baby in. And you have to let me know everything. Phone me, OK? And don't come back empty-handed!"

⌘ ⌘ ⌘

Unathi double-locked the door of his house and stood for a minute, looking up and down the street. Parks was nowhere to be seen. With his hands deep in his pockets, he began walking casually towards Busi's house.

He clutched the key to her door in one hand, and as he walked he kept a sharp lookout for Parks's taxi.

"*Hayi* Unathi," said a familiar voice, as he turned a corner, "why are you not at school today?"

Unathi looked up. It was a neighbour, standing in her yard, hanging her wet washing on the line.

Unathi paused, thinking fast, and then he smiled broadly. "It's exam time, Auntie," he said confidently, "we go in later. I only write at 10 o'clock today. So I'm just getting some fresh air." Unathi breathed deeply. "I need it after all that studying."

Auntie frowned at him, clutching a wet shirt, the water dripping down onto the ground. Unathi could see her mind ticking over. She probably didn't believe him. She was the suspicious type. Unathi knew his father would hear about this when he came home. Oh well, he thought, walking on, I'll deal with that later.

Unathi was getting closer to Busi's house. He kept checking for Parks's taxi, and for the lurking presence of Parks himself.

With relief Unathi arrived at Busi's front door, and after a final check of the road, he slipped the key into the lock, opened the door, and moved into the dim interior of the shack.

Unathi shut the door and looked around. The house was just as Busi had left it. Her bed was unmade, the sheets stripped off and lying in a pile next to the bed. Drawers were pulled out of her bedside cabinet, as if she had dressed in a hurry. Some items of clothing were lying on the floor. Unathi noticed that the cupboards in the kitchen were bare. Busi's grandmother's bed was well made and empty. On the kitchen table was a half-drunk cup of black tea and an empty plate, strewn with a few white bread crumbs.

Unathi shook his head. He opened the fridge. It was empty.

I wonder how long this has been going on, he thought. Busi must have been starving.

He found a plastic bag and walked over to Busi's cupboard. He felt strange as he began to sort through her things, but then told himself that it was the only way. Busi was in no state to help herself and, besides, with Parks on the loose, it was too dangerous for Busi to be out and about.

Unathi had his back to the door and was gently folding some of Busi's clothing when he had the idea of using Busi's school bag. He lifted out the contents of the bag onto the bed – just a couple of school books – and packed the clothes into it. Just then he heard a noise at the front door. Unathi froze, then looked around as he heard the handle turning. It seemed to him that his heart stood still in his chest. The only place he could think to hide was under the bed.

As Unathi dropped to the floor his last thought was, why didn't I lock the door behind me? He didn't even have anything with which to defend himself against Parks. He should have heard the taxi pulling up outside. He must have come on foot. Unathi's heart raced. He needed courage.

The door opened quickly and someone stepped into the room.

"Busi!"

It was a woman's voice. Unathi looked up.

Busi's mother, Khanya! Relief flooded over Unathi as he peered at her over the top of Busi's bed. She was frowning at him, the door still standing wide open behind her.

"Close the door, Auntie," was all Unathi could think to say, adding, "Close it quickly!"

Khanya turned and did as he said. Then she turned back to Unathi, dropping her heavy suitcase on the floor as she did so. "What are you doing here, Unathi?" she asked, moving towards him as he stood up from the floor, "And where is Busi?"

Unathi sat down heavily on Busi's bed. "I'm so glad you are here, Auntie," he said, rubbing his hand over his face. "Something terrible has happened."

Unathi told Khanya all he knew about Busi's situation. Khanya listened intently, her brow furrowed. Then she turned to Unathi and said, "Let's go to her now, Unathi. Come with me. Quickly. And keep an eye out for this Parks. I don't know him, so you will have to watch out for him."

Unathi grabbed the school bag and went out of the house. He looked up and down the road. The coast was clear, and so he called

Khanya, and the two of them began walking back towards Unathi's house.

They were walking quickly, Unathi constantly looking over his shoulder, when they turned a corner and walked straight into him.

Parks.

Unathi stepped back. "Parks!" he said, shocked, looking up at the big man towering over him.

"Hello, boy," said Parks, gripping Unathi by the arm and ignoring Busi's mother. "Where are you coming from?" He pulled Unathi closer. "And where is Busi? I know you know, boy! Tell me!"

Unathi felt pain in his arm where Parks was holding him very tightly.

"Let him go," said Khanya as she laid her hand against Parks's chest and pushed. Parks did not move an inch, but he glared at her for a minute. Then, choosing to ignore her, he looked back at Unathi.

"I said, let him go!" said Khanya. Parks ignored her, and Khanya continued speaking, raising her voice. "I don't think you know who I am," said Khanya, her voice steady and strong.

Parks looked back at Khanya, who stood, frowning angrily at him, her arms folded across her chest.

"I am the mother of Busi," she said. "I am Khanya … and you, yes, I know you. You are Parks!" Khanya paused as Parks released Unathi, and turned towards her.

"You are the man who made my under-age daughter pregnant, are you not?"

Parks blinked, and was about to speak, but Khanya silenced him. She put up her hand, and shook her head.

"Get out of my way, Mister," she said, as she took Unathi's hand. "I have no time for you now. Come, Unathi!"

Khanya and Unathi strode in the direction of Unathi's house, neither looking back at Parks. He stood as if glued to the ground, his mouth hanging open.

Suddenly Khanya whirled around. "And you'd better keep away from my daughter!" she shouted, as they walked away. "I am here now. Busi is not alone any more. Keep away from us all!"

Unathi was impressed. After a few paces he looked back. Parks was still there, looking after them. But he had made no move to follow them.

Just before they turned the corner Unathi saw Parks unlocking his taxi and climbing in. For a moment Unathi thought he was going to follow them, but then the taxi drove off in the opposite direction.

He and Khanya walked on to Unathi's house, and after looking around one more time, Unathi unlocked and opened the door.

Chapter 19

"Mama!"

Busi flew into her mother's arms when she saw her walking through the front door. The two women clung to each other, both of them sobbing. Unathi stood awkwardly by, grinning. He dropped Busi's school bag and went to put the kettle on.

When he came back into the room, carrying two cups of strong, sweet tea, he was surprised to see Busi and Khanya standing far apart. Busi looked angry.

"Busi," Khanya was saying to her daughter with her arms outstretched, "please let me explain why …"

"No," said Busi fiercely, "I don't want to hear now. You're too late. And it's all your fault …" Busi's voice trailed off, and she sank down into a chair and dropped her head into her hands.

Busi's mother approached her slowly, speaking soothingly. "I understand how you must feel, my child," she said softly, "and maybe later there will be time for me to tell you why I could not come before."

Khanya stood behind Busi and put her hand on Busi's shoulder. "For now you must tell me one thing, Busi," she said, stroking Busi's shoulder slowly. "Where is your baby, my child?"

Busi pulled away, and lifted her face, wet with tears.

"She's safe, she's alive." Busi took a deep breath, and then sighed, looking away from her mother. "You are too late, Mama. Too late. You took too long to come. And I didn't think you would want me to keep the baby, anyway."

Khanya stood in silence, her head drooping.

Busi turned and looked up at her. "Why didn't you come, Mama? I begged you to come. For so long …" Then Busi looked away.

Khanya turned to Unathi and took the cups of tea from him. She gave one to Busi, who absent-mindedly took it, and sipped from it. Khanya pulled a chair closer to Busi and sat down.

"Listen Busi," she said, leaning closer to her daughter, "and I will tell you."

Busi remained silent as her mother spoke. Occasionally she would raise her tear-filled eyes to Khanya as she mentioned some or other fact.

Gradually she allowed her mother to reach over and touch her hands, still stained with mud.

"Your father left me for another woman very soon after we arrived in Jozi," began Busi's mother. Then she looked down, paused and drank deeply from her cup of tea. "It wasn't long before he moved away from me and went to live with her. He had his job already, but that woman took all his money. He gave none to me. I had a few cleaning jobs, but I struggled to find full-time work. I begged him for money to send back to you and Gogo, but it was like he didn't care. He thought only of her."

Unathi shifted uneasily and moved away to his bedroom, leaving the two women alone.

Khanya continued. "I didn't want to tell you, Busi. I knew it would break your heart. Just like mine was being broken. I kept hoping for better work. I kept hoping that your father's heart would soften. I prayed so hard for that." Khanya looked up at her daughter. "But it never did. I sent you what I could. I should have told you and Gogo both the truth. I see that now."

Busi looked up at her mother and held her gaze.

Khanya continued. "When I heard that you had fallen pregnant, I felt desperate. I did not want to tell your father. I thought he would get angry and that would make the situation worse. But when my mother got so sick I went to him. I begged him. I begged him."

Khanya fell silent. Softly she said, "Thank God his heart softened a little then. He promised to help me come home." Khanya shrugged her shoulders and a little smile played on her lips. "And here I am, my daughter. Here I am."

Busi leant towards her mother and her mother leant towards her, and they held each other tightly for a long while.

"But Gogo is dying, Mama," said Busi, looking up into her mothers' face. "She is so very sick."

"No," said Busi's mother, looking down at Busi, and shaking her head, "that's not so. I went to the hospital before I came here. She's going to be all right, Busi. I've seen her. She really will be all right. She will come home again."

Busi couldn't believe it. She smiled at her mother through her tears, and allowed her mother to wipe her wet cheeks. Khanya stood up, walked to the school bag and picked it up.

"Now," she said firmly, "you need a good wash, my child. Wash yourself clean and put on clean clothes, and then we can talk."

Khanya called Unathi and he led them to the bathroom. Khanya turned on the taps and mother and daughter stood deep in thought as the water ran into the bath and the white, frothy bubbles rose high out of the water. Then Khanya smiled lovingly at Busi, gave her a towel and left the bathroom, shutting the door behind her.

She found Unathi sitting in the lounge, staring though the window. She knew what he was thinking. For Khanya too it was a burning question: where was Busi's baby?

Chapter 20

Parks lurched up the path, dreading having to open the door and face Thandi's rages and tears. The paving stones were playing tricks on him and he stumbled. He couldn't remember how many whiskys he had knocked back at the tavern to drown his feelings of shame and humiliation.

Thandi rushed to the door as he opened it. "The baby's bottle," she said. "All warm and ready. Where is the baby?"

"Busi's mother was there," he said. "And I couldn't see the baby anywhere."

"You were always a quitter!" Thandi screamed at Parks. "You should have forced them to give it to you."

"I don't know where it is, Thandi. It's gone. And they're watching out for us. It's over."

Thandi gripped his arm and squeezed it. She was surprisingly strong. "We will watch. We will go to her house and we will take the baby when she is out."

Those words sobered Parks up. He remembered the last terrible scene when Thandi had come home with a baby. Someone else's baby. Luckily it had been sorted out, and they had not pressed charges. But it had been a close thing.

"Thandi. We can't take it. Remember what happened last time."

"This is different. This baby is yours."

"But, Thandi, she is the mother, she–"

"You're not listening to me!" Thandi shouted. She threw the baby's bottle onto the floor, and it bounced and rolled under the table. "You bring me that baby or else you're out!" She headed towards the glasses. Last time she had flown into a rage with him she had broken them all. He grabbed her, pulled her back.

"Thandi! Her mother mentioned the police! You don't want that again! Remember when they locked you up for the night!"

He could see his words had hit home. Her face crumpled. "You're so selfish," she said. "You would have got the baby if you cared for me. You don't love me – you just use me for my money."

"That's not true, darling," said Parks, stroking her cheek. But it sounded unconvincing, even to him. How had he landed up like this?

He should have taken it as a warning when Thandi's uncle had hardly wanted *lobola*. He had just wanted the marriage to go ahead, even though they were both so young and hardly knew each other. And then he had discovered after the wedding that Thandi was three months pregnant.

Parks had been furious, even more so when Thandi wouldn't tell him who the father was. But he had had his suspicions. Thandi had been brought up by an aunt who never went out of the house, and an uncle who threw money at Thandi as if he was paying for some terrible sin. When Thandi's uncle had died a few weeks later and left them his money, Thandi had refused to go to his funeral. That's when he knew what the uncle had done.

But he, Parks, had still felt lucky. He had never imagined being rich. And now here he was with lots of money. It had felt like his life was beginning again. He had even accepted that he was going to be father to another man's child.

Then the accident had happened …

Thandi started to cry.

"I need that baby," she said, "and I need you to get it for me. Otherwise I don't know what I will do."

"It's going to be OK," said Parks, as he fetched her a drink and soothed her. He felt a deep relief that her rage, like a storm, had passed. She would not kick him out, at least not now.

"You are so good to me, Parks – I don't deserve you," she said. "We will be a real family soon, with a baby, and everything will be different, I promise."

Chapter 21

Unathi had made scrambled eggs and sausage for them all by the time Busi came out of the bathroom. They sat down together around the table and ate hungrily, washing the meal down with large cups of tea.

When the table was cleared and the plates had been cleaned and put away, Khanya turned to Unathi. "Busi has told me where her baby is," she said in a clear voice, turning to smile gently at Busi.

Busi sat quite still, and looked down at her hands. She was frowning, and Unathi could see tears gathering at the corners of her eyes.

"I am so proud of you," said Khanya gently, sitting down next to Busi on the sofa and putting her arm around her. "You made a very brave and difficult decision. You put your baby first, and made sure that she would be safe and taken care of."

Then Khanya stood up, and turned to Unathi. "I know you should be at school,

Unathi, and I am very grateful for everything that you have done for Busi today. There's just one more thing I need to ask you to do."

Unathi stepped forward, clasping his hands together in front of him. "It's nothing, Auntie," he said with a shrug. "During exams most kids stay at home anyway when they're not writing. I have no exam to write today." Then Unathi smiled at Busi, and added, "I'm just really glad you ran into me today, Busi. I wish you had asked me for help earlier."

"But I thought you–" She stopped.

"What?" he asked.

"Nothing," she said. "Nothing at all."

"So," said Khanya, gathering her handbag and putting on her jacket, "Can Busi stay here with you for a few hours?"

Unathi nodded. "She will be safe here."

Khanya moved towards the door, stopping on her way to look at Busi. "Things are different now, Busi. I am back for good. Together we will deal with everything."

Busi looked up her mother and nodded.

Khanya continued, "And Gogo will be coming home soon as well." Then, smiling broadly, she said, "Don't worry, Busi. We will get your baby back, you'll see. And together the three of us will cope absolutely fine."

With that Khanya opened the front door and went out.

After Busi's mother had left Unathi glanced towards Busi. Busi sat curled up on the sofa.

"What do you feel like doing?" asked Unathi, moving to the television. "Shall we watch?"

Busi nodded, and Unathi put on the television.

Busi and Unathi sat together and watched some shows. Unathi spoke every now and then, to tell Busi some bit of gossip about school. Busi listened and smiled. She was so happy that Unathi was here with her, looking at her like he used to. But her thoughts were also far away, with a small baby girl wrapped in a fluffy pink blanket.

⌘ ⌘ ⌘

A few hours passed. Unathi had turned off the television and sat quietly next to Busi, who had fallen asleep on the sofa. He was startled by the sound of voices and footsteps approaching his front door.

He stood up and moved the curtains a little so that he could peer out. He was relieved to see Khanya and another woman walking up the path to the front door.

Quickly Unathi opened the door. "You're back," he said. "Busi is sleeping."

Khanya led the way in. "Yes," she said, nodding towards her companion behind her, "and this is the social worker dealing with Busi's baby. Busi has had a very exhausting time. It's good that she is sleeping."

Just then Busi sat up, startled, her eyes still blurry with sleep. She had heard her mother's voice.

"Do you have her?" she asked. "Mama, where is my baby?" Seeing her mother's arms empty, she looked frantically around, then sprang up and ran towards the door.

Khanya took Busi by the hand before she got through the door and hugged her tight.

"It's all right, Busi," she said gently, "We are going to take you to your baby now. Everything is going to be all right."

⌘ ⌘ ⌘

Unathi, Ntombi, Lettie and Asanda waited at Busi's house for her to arrive home with her baby. They had gathered together some gifts: a beautiful top and some fragrant hand cream for Busi, and a pack of three babygros and baby vests for the baby. Asanda blew up a few balloons.

"Just make sure you don't pop any," said Lettie with some concern. "We don't want to terrify the little thing."

"You're right," said Ntombi, with a shake of her head. "She's had an adventurous enough start to her life already."

Busi climbed out of the social worker's car and walked towards her friends, crowding the door of her home. The girls came forward and gathered around her, all peering excitedly at the baby held tightly in Busi's arms.

"Oh," said Ntombi gleefully, "she's so gorgeous."

"Let me hold her," said Lettie, edging forward, and reaching eagerly for the baby.

"Just a minute, girls," said Khanya, putting her arm around Busi, and guiding her inside.

Once inside, the baby was passed from one girl to the next, and they all kissed her soft brown cheeks and wondered at the size of her tiny hands and fingers.

Then the baby started crying. "Here," said Asanda quickly, "over to you."

Busi tried to rock her, but the crying just got louder.

"Let me take her," said Unathi. He picked the crying baby up and started dancing around the room with her.

"Be careful," said Busi. But she saw that he was holding the baby safely and steadily, even as he danced around. Almost instantly the baby quietened. Unathi slowed down. The baby started crying again.

The girls collapsed with laughter. "You're going to have to do that all day, Unathi," said Ntombi.

Unathi suddenly made a face, and came quickly to Busi. "She's done something in her nappy. I'm afraid I can't help with that."

Busi's mother took the baby and, laying her on a towel on the sofa, cleaned her expertly. "She needs feeding soon," she said to Busi.

Busi sighed. Having a baby was a full-time job.

"Before you do that, come and say goodbye. Mrs Mbewu is leaving," said her mother.

They started walking out to the street.

"All of us at St Saviour's Church will be here to help you as much as we can," Mrs Mbewu said, lifting a large hamper of nappies and baby clothes from the back seat of her car. "We didn't have her with us for very long, but we all fell in love with her. I will come back tomorrow to make sure everything is all right."

"What do we do if Parks comes?" asked Busi.

The social worker shook her head and turned to Khanya. "I'm sure he will stay away now. I traced him and told him he could be facing a charge. He has received summons to appear in court on a charge of statutory rape, as Busi wasn't 16 yet when they had sex."

Busi looked down, embarrassed at these words in front of her mother. But the social worker continued. "Apparently his wife is also on their books, as she assaulted a mother with a baby in a supermarket last month. If they harrass you, or try to take the baby, we will help you to get a protection order against him."

"Thank you, Mrs Mbewu. Thank you so much," said Busi. "I feel so much safer knowing that you are here for me if I need you."

"Busi, the baby's crying!" Ntombi called, and Busi shook the social worker's hand and thanked her one more time and went back inside.

"I am glad to see Busi so happy. Now are *you* going to be all right, Khanya?" the social worker asked.

"My mother will be coming home next week," said Khanya, "and I will find some work very soon. I know I will."

"We can help you with that," said the social worker, getting into her car. "And next year Busi can go back to school to finish Matric."

Khanya waved goodbye as the social worker drove away. Then she turned and walked

143

towards the open door of her house, where she could see Busi's friends sitting around the table. Her daughter was not there – she must be feeding her baby behind the curtain.

Busi heard her mother's voice as she walked in, heard her friends' excited chatter and laughter. She looked down at her baby and smiled. I know my life will not be easy with a newborn child, she thought to herself. But now my tears have dried and my heart is overflowing with hope. That will be your name, my little one. Thembisa. Hope in Xhosa. Because after the tears came hope.